Gayatri is a therapist, poet, and author. Her previous works include *Anitya, Sit Your Self Down*, and *Who Me, Poor?*.

Gayatri holds a Nalanda Diploma and is a student of the Nalanda Masters in Buddhist Philosophy, both under the aegis of His Holiness the Dalai Lama. She is a practitioner of Vipassana, and the Ngondro Gar under Dzongsar Khyentse Rinpoche. She studied Vedic Culture and Spirituality and Indian Philosophy at Sri Satya Sai Institute of Higher Learning, Puttaparthi. She holds postgraduate degrees in English literature, journalism, counselling psychology and Buddhist psychology.

She has worked in the Indian media for 22 years and is a mental health columnist for MoneyControl. Her non-fiction work has appeared in the *Hindustan Times, India Today*, and *Mint Lounge* and as part of an award-winning anthology of *Out of Print* edited by with Meena Kandasamy and Samhita Arni. Her poetry had been shortlisted for the Bridport Prize 2021 and featured in the Converse Anthology commemorating 75 years of Indian Independence in 2022, among others. She's lived in Lagos (Nigeria), Kodaikanal (Tamil Nadu), and Thane (Maharashtra). She is the founder of Shamah | शाम: a mind-body-spirit alignment practice.

This is a beautifully written book for children, making them expectantly wait for the sequel.

–Bibek Debroy, Author, Translator, Economist

How do we teach our children to reach for the skies while being rooted in tradition? How do we help our children to reflect and think through their emotions? Gayatri's wonder-filled fable about a young girl called Devi, her joys and sorrows, and her nine companions does this in great style. An adventure story set in the present that anyone who has dreamt of being elsewhere will enjoy, identify with, and learn from. A love letter to childhood, day dreams, and imagination.

–Keerthik Sasidharan, Author, *The Dharma Forest*

A delight to read, a book for all ages!

Gayatri has wrought an extraordinary, fantastical tale of coming to terms with loss and loneliness in which the navarasas, the nine emotions, manifest as guiding companions.

This tale is woven with familial love, and brings to mind the crazy, comic malevolence of Roald Dahl while drawing on ideas inspired by our epics. This is a story for India and the world of the here and now.

Indira Chandrashekhar, Scientist, Author,
and Founder of *Out of Print*

Devi & the Battle of Meghadhanush

A Rasa Bhugola Story

Gayatri

Om Books International

First published in 2023 by

Om Books International

Corporate & Editorial Office
A-12, Sector 64, Noida 201 301
Uttar Pradesh, India
Phone: +91 120 477 4100
Email: editorial@ombooks.com
Website: www.ombooksinternational.com

Sales Office
107, Ansari Road, Darya Ganj,
New Delhi 110 002, India
Phone: +91 11 4000 9000
Email: sales@ombooks.com
Website: www.ombooks.com

ISBN: 978-93-95701-05-1

Printed in India

10 9 8 7 6 5 4 3 2 1

The Butterfly Guide to the Navarasas

Shanta	Tranquility	Eternal White	Air
Hasya	Mirth	White + Silver Gold & Rose Glitter (Insignia of the Messenger)	Fire
Adbhuta	Wonder	Yellow	Fire
Sringara	Love	Light Green	Water
Vira	Courage	Saffron	Water
Vibhatsa	Aversion	Blue	Water
Karunya	Compassion	Grey	Water
Raudra	Fury	Red	Fire
Bhayanaka	Terror	Black	Air

Contents

FOR

Dhruv,
Anushka, Mihika,
Biko, Tutu, Erika,
Vihaan, & Niranthara

May the rasas be your guide

Chapter 1

What's the Password?

No matter how fast she gave chase, it always remained just out of reach. She stretched out across an unbridgeable gap. Between her and it, lay an unanswerable riddle.

Her wings shimmer with the moods of day, from a moonlit midnight to the white-out of deep noon. She is both there and not there. Grasp her, she disappears. She is born where water, air, and fire meet. Her presence both alters everything and leaves it unchanged. Who is she?

Every time she neared an answer, the chimera dissolved.

Devi stirred from her dream to hear the front door shut with a gentle click. The house fell to that all-familiar stillness that rose like a catch in her throat when she was on her own again. She knew it well. She hadn't stirred when Pa had stood at the door and said, "Bye Devi, I know you can hear me!" and blew noisy kisses in her direction. She only vaguely heard Mom rummage through her cupboard and lay out her uniform for the day, her instructions droning on in the background.

This is how it was, and had been for some time now. Ammamma had passed a year ago, and until then, she had been Devi's constant companion. Ammamma told her funny stories about her father being so bad at maths that he just left entire rows of numbers out of sums if he didn't like them. Of Mom's cooking disasters and how she burned herself till she was hopping across the kitchen with band aids across all her fingers. Ammamma and Devi had laughed till they cried. "Ammamma's Ammunition" Pa had called his Amma's stories. They were particularly potent whenever Devi was being scolded about homework gone wrong, or for poor test scores, or for not finishing one of her chores. Ammamma would just raise the shield. "And what about when you got sent out of class a whole week in a row for not doing your homework, hunh?" she would say indignantly, her hands on her hips and one raised eyebrow. Ammamma knew everybody's secrets and she wasn't afraid to use them. She was a quick draw too. Devi would immediately get behind her, Ammamma's small but fierce frame her living body armour. Pa would look at his Amma, thunder in his eyes, and say, "Stop loading her with ammo, Amma." Ammamma and Devi would just glance at each other and start giggling and then no one in the room could stay mad for long.

Now, with Ammamma gone, there was no one to protect Devi anymore. At eleven and a half, she was old enough not to need too much supervision, and her parents didn't think it was safe to admit an unknown person into the house at this stage. Besides, it was only half an hour in the morning. Devi just had to wake up, get dressed, eat her breakfast and leave for school. Mom laid everything out for her, from socks and shoes to the packed lunch and school bag by the door. Devi also got in about an hour earlier than Mom in the evening, and again there was always a snack and a chocolate milk in the fridge. All Devi had to do was pull the door behind her.

That really wasn't it, right? Just having all the things Devi needed there, laid out, somehow made it seem even more lonely to Devi. As though Ammamma was replaceable with just the things she used to do. It seemed like so not the point, but they didn't get that. No one did. Ever since then, whenever Devi got upset, she would cause an earthquake. Only in her head, but she found it useful. If she concentrated really hard and clenched her teeth, Devi found she could allow her hands and her feet to tremble. She imagined she was uprooting the whole world. It was only for a moment, in her mind. Everything went down. All the trees and buildings and parks and schools, all the roads and stores, until there was nothing left. Then she could allow it all to return to normal. Then she felt much more in control.

"What mischief can she possibly be up to?" Mom said to Pa, who just shrugged and replied, "I don't want to find out."

The alternative would be Mom staying home from work, and they agreed, after much discussion in raised voices, that they needed the double income. So, it was decided: Devi would be alone at home for a half hour every morning and an hour every evening. They even put in an alphanumeric lock at the front door so she wouldn't have to carry a key. All she had to do was type in her birthday, which she couldn't possibly forget, to get in and out of the house, and not reveal it to anyone.

She was what they called 'a big girl now', and Devi discovered that being 'a big girl' meant mostly being on your own.

"Think of it as an adventure," Mom said to her.

"Just don't try and make it one," Pa had warned.

"I'm just going to sleep and miss the bus," Devi had shrugged. It would be their fault and they would get phone calls from the school.

That's when Mom came up with the ingenious microwave beeping idea. She had read about a famous musician whose wife used to play a few opening notes on the piano and he would be so annoyed at the incomplete tune that he would have to drag himself out of bed and complete it by playing the rest of it. Well, they didn't have a piano and Devi was no musician, but voila! The microwave-piano served the double function of heating the food and dragging her out of bed because it was that one sound Devi found so annoying.

There it went now. Arrrgh!! It was so aggravating!

As if it wasn't enough to have to fetch everything you needed on your own, dress yourself, and actually show up at school every day, Devi was being hauled up too. She had to have steady test scores, to finish her homework, and do her chores, like make her own bed, put her worn clothes into the washing machine after her bath and press the button to switch it on. Mom had shown her how. She had had to, exasperatedly! Ammamma had secretly taken all these on for Devi over these years. She had to 'come on, grow up, be a big girl' constantly now.

"Get up silly, they've gone now," Ammamma's voice came to her now.

Devi shot out of her bedclothes like she'd found a rat in them.

"Who said that?" she asked, her chest thumping like a Ganesh Chaturthi procession winding its way to the beach front. But the question rattled around the empty home.

"Who's there?" she asked again, grabbing her pillow in self defence, because, you know, pillows are what you build forts with for a reason.

No answer.

Devi sighed in relief and conked herself on the head for good measure. She was talking to herself again. She creeped herself out when she did that.

She could hear the hum of the fridge and the whirring of the dishwasher. Her breakfast in the microwave was beeping like a lost lamb.

Devi swung her legs around, dangling them off the edge, and sat up in bed, ready to start her day. From the window she could see the colony gate, where school buses and vans were drawing up to pick up kindergarteners, with nannies, Moms and Pas waving them off till the bus left. She could see grandparents walking in circles in the garden, some of them friends of her Ammamma. They still waved to her and nodded knowingly as she made her way to the stop. They missed her too. She avoided them sometimes, when the heaviness in her heart became too much, as though she were a balloon with a stone tied to the end of its thread that was trailing along the ground. She looked up at the flats in the building opposite hers, nearer her 14th floor one. In some, the Pas had left for work but the Moms were sipping tea or chopping vegetables while the cleaning ladies made their way methodically through the house, sweeping or swabbing or flicking the clothes out as they put them to dry. Devi never understood how the clothes didn't fall off the washing lines that hung so precariously on what looked to her like two arms stretched out, so high up. Devi got her toothbrush and stood at the glass balcony door forlornly brushing her teeth, splattering all over the door, just as Mom warned her so many times not to do. Sometimes when she was alone, she thought of things Mom wouldn't want her to do just so she could go do them. Not enough to get a scolding but just enough to leave a hint that she was really really *really* mad at them.

A chameleon ran along the balcony railing and stopped to stare at her and nod.

Devi blinked twice. It seemed to be wearing some sort of a scarf, Devi could swear. Perhaps someone's washing, a sock or something, had become entangled around its neck. But it scampered off before she could blink the sleep out of her eyes and look again.

Devi turned around to see if anyone else had seen it. And that's when it hit her that there was no one around to say these little things to.

Devi felt quite invisible sometimes.

"HELLLOOO I'M ALL ALONE HERE," she shouted.

"Ouch! Not so loud," Ammamma's voice said.

Devi's brush fell from her hand. She watched it leave a long streak down the glass door and stain the rug. Mom would really be mad now.

"That's okay, as long as you don't think you are," the voice came again.

"Are what?" Devi asked out loud this time.

"Mad, of course," the voice said, and went off into a peal of laughter.

Devi was sure of it. Only Ammamma laughed at her own jokes that much.

"Ammamma?" she asked, nervously looking around the room.

"Are you?"

"Am I what?"

"Sure of it? Are you sure you're mad or are you sure you're not mad?"

"Ammamma is that you?" she said again, hoping it was, then quickly, hoping it wasn't.

Devi got on her knees to pick up her brush. "There you go again, this and that, that and this, always unsure."

The bed! The voice was coming from under the bed!

Devi bent down and peeped under her bed.

"Over here," the voice said.

Devi reached for her phone, shook it until the torch on it came on, and shone it into the corners.

"Can't see anything."

"Of course not silly, you haven't said the password," the voice said.

Devi frowned. "What password?"

"Ah, that would be telling, wouldn't it?"

The microwave beeped again. Devi remembered she was getting late for school. This delay was not one she would be able to explain away easily.

"Why are you late Devi?"

"Miss, I was talking to a voice under the bed."

"Really, what did the voice say?"

"It asked me for a password, Miss."

That would be a no-return-ticket trip to the school counsellor.

"Hyakhyakhyakhyakhyakhyaak," the voice chuckled.

"Oh my god, you even laugh like her," Devi said.

Devi wondered if she should just go back to bed and try waking up again.

"What makes you so sure I'm in your dream?" the voice said. "How do you know you're not in mine?"

Devi thought about it and went into a loopity loop of whose dream it was. Perhaps, she thought, they were in each other's dreams. What if they couldn't wake up until they had the password?

"I really can't tell you the password, you know," the voice said kindly.

"Then how would I know it?" Devi demanded.

"It's something your Ammamma would have already told you. Think, think!"

Devi sat back, leaned against the wall, and frowned.

What were the words Ammamma used to teach her?

"Kuzhandai?" which is what she called her affectionately.

"Pottu? Specs?" which were things she used to keep searching for, asking Devi to find.

"Kudharai vaal?" which is what she used to call Devi's ponytail.

"I'm sorry, are you saying something or babbling like a baby?"

Devi burst out laughing.

"No, I'm just thinking of all the words Ammamma used to say."

"Well, considering that an average human speaks around 125 words a minute, maybe just randomly thinking of all the words a person spoke in their lifetime is a bit broad. You may want to narrow that down? I haven't got forever you know..."

"You don't? How long have you got then?"

The voice dropped its pitch a little.

"Um... a little less than forever... Oh, hurry up!"

"WHY can't you just TELL me the password? And don't you roll your eyes at me!"

"I swear I didn't roll my eyes."

"Yes, you did."

"You don't know that."

"Of course, I do. I can sense it. Come on, this is silly!"

"Well, it's for security you know, so *they* can't find me."

"Who *they*? There's only me here."

"Look, I know they're your parents and all, but you know... *the grown-ups...*"

"Oh them. Pfft. Never mind them. If I disappeared while I was sitting at the dinner table talking to them, they wouldn't notice."

"Awwww, not true at all, I'm sure they would."

"Believe me, I've been a disembodied voice longer than you have been one."

"I'm rolling my eyes now."

"I can tell."

"Really? How?"

"I dunno, something in the air..."

"Anyway, point is, it's forbidden to reveal it. I would lose my wings."

"Oooh you have wings? What colour?"

"If you could see me, you'd know. You don't catch on very quickly, do you?"

"OK shush, let me crack the password."

The microwave beeped again.

"Oh shoot, I'm going to miss my bus for sure today."

"Does it matter?"

Devi looked at herself in the mirror. She was on her knees, her teeth half brushed, her head covered in dust bunnies from under the bed, with the torchlight from her mobile phone still on, speaking to a voice that sounded like her dead grandmother. She probably had more important appointments to handle than the one with her bus.

What was that Ammamma used to say? "When you don't know what you feel like doing, go and have a bath and then you'll know."

"This might work better if I got ready first," Devi said to the voice.

"Sure, I get it."

Devi went to the bathroom and freshened up. She then pulled on a fresh pair of shorts and her old favourite Mr Men t-shirt that mom was always threatening to throw away but was just the perfect level of soft. Then, she went to the kitchen to stop the godawful beeping machine. She switched on the television, more so that there would be some sound in the house. It was set to the National Geographic channel.

Devi walked around the house chewing her *poha* thoughtfully, thinking about Ammamma and not even noticing she hadn't added the strands of crunchy *sev* and the curd or squeezed the slice of lemon that Mom had kept out for her to go along with it, just the way she usually liked it. Then she absent-mindedly put down her bowl somewhere and forgot where she put it. She didn't feel like drinking her milk so she took a spoon to the Bournvita jar and began to eat it instead, because wasn't that the same thing really?

All she could think of was all the things Ammamma would say.

"Ammamma chummama?"

"I thought you would say that to her?"

"Ayyo kaddavule?" which meant 'Oh Gawd' in Ammamma speak.

The voice just sighed now. Just the way Ammamma would have sighed.

The phone rang, it was Mom. She was calling to confirm if Devi was on track for the bus.

"Hyakhyakhyakhyakhyakhyaak," the voice went. Devi was absolutely not on track. She was so far off track she couldn't see where the track was.

This time Devi chuckled along. "Yeah, I know right."

Oh, there was no way to explain her way out of this one. She was in *so* much trouble.

She ran on the spot as she picked up the call. She was huffing and panting.

"Yes Mom, just leaving. Call you in the evening," she said, trying to sound as hurried as she could, and cut the call before Mom had a chance to ask any questions.

Devi fetched a pen and an old notebook, and sat down cross-legged on the rug. Then she began to scribble down all the things Ammamma used to say as fast as she could remember them. From boring everyday stuff like 'your milk is going cold' to all her magnificent proverbs like 'what does a donkey know about the taste of ginger' that she was always muttering. Between that and keeping up with the hibernation patterns of bears, by the time she looked up, it was well past noon and she was hungry again. She pulled her lunchbox out of her bag. There were tomato, cheese and basil sandwiches today. She also found a stash of chips in a kitchen cupboard and some chocolate-chip cookies. She poured herself some soda out of the fridge and managed to microwave some frozen French fries, squirting them with nacho cheese. Later, she would allow herself some ice cream out of the freezer. It was a veritable feast. She thought of her classmates slogging it out in class and swallowing cold rotis on the playground.

Sometime during the tale of the unique friendship of the rhino and the red-billed oxpecker, Devi dozed off on the sofa, the remains of her feast strewn around her, like a jackal in the remains of a wildebeest.

The butterfly streaked across her mind's eye, leaving the residue of a rainbow lingering in its dappled sky. Somewhere in the background, Ammamma's voice, sitting in front of her altar, muttering her morning chants arose. The sun's rays filtered in through the open window.

Devi woke up with a jerk. She remembered. There *was* one place she hadn't looked for an answer.

She raced to Ammamma's bedroom but an old memory made her trip over her own feet. She hesitated at the door. Devi hadn't been inside since she had passed away. The room still smelled of Ammamma; a mixture of sandalwood soap and talcum powder, dried rose petals and the mothballs in her saris, the smell of old crinkly pages with scripts, and of faded ink in letters that she couldn't read... The room smelled like a locked-up corner of her heart.

Devi felt like she'd swallowed a lump of sugar as she entered the room. It was neatly made up, though all of Ammamma's things that had been on her nightstand and in front of her mirror had been put away into neat boxes or given away. There were just all her pictures of gods and goddesses on her little altar, just as she had left them. Mom lit a lamp now and then on special days and festivals, but for the most part they just kept a small yellow bulb switched on there instead. An old calendar fluttered on a wall, and on the wall behind the bed, hung a painting. It had been Ammamma's favourite.

Devi lay down on her back on the bed, upside down so her feet were on the pillow and her head at the foot. What was it Ammamma used to say? Ulta-pulta girl! Devi loved to lie that way because she could gaze at the painting. It seemed mesmerising to her.

"Otherwise, what is the point, Ammamma?" Devi would ask.

So, Ammamma would also lay her head at the foot of the bed and they would pick out patterns in the painting. Devi loved it for the same reason as Ammamma. Because every time you looked at it, it looked different. It had a life of its own.

The painting was simply the most amazing thing Devi had ever seen. It felt like magic, real magic to her, the way a painting so full of wonder could come alive in your mind's eye when it was no longer in front of you.

Everything in it was yellow. And as long as Anil Appappan was alive, Ammamma used to say, everything in her life was sunny and bright.

When she came from Goa to Mumbai to live with them after Anil Appappan had died, the painting was the only thing of any real value she had brought with her apart from her clothes. She gave away everything else, all her jewels and kitchen stores and the furniture in the house, to her daughters.

Devi hadn't realised it, but as she thought of this now, tears had begun to flow from her eyes.

She had loved looking at it once, but after Ammamma had passed away, it was like that time was gone. Instead of making her happy, it now made her sad, so she had stopped coming into the room and she had stopped gazing at the painting.

She caught the glint out of the corner of her eye, emerging from a swirling haze.

The outline of a wing, a gentle shimmer, a flutter, an afternoon breeze, the tinkling of tiny bells.

Then, the chimera dispersed as quickly as it had appeared.

"That's it! That's it!" the voice shouted, excitedly.

"What? What? Tell me!" Devi said.

"What you were thinking about. I felt a buzzy warm glow. Try it again."

"The painting?"

"Yes, yes, see it happened again!"

It felt like the dream all over again. It was there, Devi was here, and in the middle, an unsolvable riddle.

The more Devi contemplated the painting, something golden flashed, the contours of the painting shimmered, flickering at the edges of the brushstrokes with pin pricks of light, and then it all went flat again, like soda with the lid left off for too long.

It all went still and dark again, just as it had been before.

Devi was disappointed, and lay back on the bed, spreading her arms wide.

She stared at the ceiling.

"It's hopeless," she thought. "Maybe I have gone utterly mad," she said.

"Noooo, don't give up now. You're almost there. I can feel it."

"Why am I talking to you anyway," said Devi, addressing the ceiling fan.

"Over here, I'm down here," the voice said.

"How does it matter? Here, there, I can't see you anyway. What's the use? This is hopeless."

"Think Devi, think, was there something you did with her in this room? Maybe something you sang or chanted, are you leaving something out?"

Devi sat up.

"Yeah, Ammamma used to make me say my morning prayer."

"Try it now!"

Devi sat up cross-legged, pretzeling one leg into the other and falling over once, but trying not to giggle. Somehow the moment seemed, well, momentous. This was it; she could feel it.

She closed her eyes.

"Oh wait," she thought. "Ammamma would make me open my eyes and look into my palms." She opened them and held her palms before her.

"Auuuuuuuuuuuummmmmmmmmmm..." she chanted.

A tiny flicker of light appeared on the outer ridges.

"Karagre vasate Lakshmi"

A gleam of translucent gold hovered over her palms.

"Karamule Saraswati"

Devi gasped as the outline of a butterfly's wings shimmered to life in a gentle silver.

"Karamadhye sthitaha Gauri"

A rose-tinted flash arose from the middle and spread outwards towards the edges, filling in the contours and details of the butterfly – speckles and dots, lines and veins.

"Prabhate kara darshanam"

Devi's hands fell away into her lap as the silver-gold and rose-gold butterfly flapped its wings and began to stir into the air. The room sparkled with flashes from the flutter and streaks of light began to swirl around Devi.

She was not scared she noticed, and wondered if she should be. How could she feel anything but awe and wonder as this beautiful creature with long tendrilous antennae and gossamer wings trembled into being? Devi watched, wonderstruck, as the beautiful creature took a turn around the room, leaving a trail of stardust and shimmer behind it.

Devi followed its flight, turning around in the middle of the room, until it suddenly flickered like a tube light and disappeared, leaving her twirling like a carousel in Ammamma's now empty room, devoid of mysterious creatures and quite ordinary looking. As she twirled, the fiercely frowning face of her mother came into sight at the doorway. And it sucked all the light right out of the room.

Mom had just travelled through the house to the end of the corridor. The floor of the living room was strewn with scribbled and torn chits of paper. She had found a bowl of half-eaten poha in the bookshelf and an empty ice cream box on the shoe cabinet. The now hardened remnants of the Bournvita jar lay on the sofa. Devi's open school bag was dumped in the corner. Her lunch box lay on her bed, which had absolutely not been made, not even half-heartedly. A trail of her nightclothes and the towel formed a path to the washroom. The balcony door in Devi's room was streaked with paste and splatter.

It occurred to Devi, purely based on Mom's expression of absolute horror dawning like a dark moon rising on the horizon, that it would not be a good idea to ask what was wrong.

Not good. So not good.

Devi glanced desperately around for the Ammamma voice or butterfly, for hello, this was the time! She could use some celestial or ethereal help out here right about now! But the butterfly was nowhere in sight. Not so much as a shimmer or a sparkle. Just the dulling light of early evening. Devi could hear the television droning on somewhere in the distance. She had forgotten to switch it off, which is why she didn't hear the door or her mother's many many *many* missed calls. *Gulp*! Devi suddenly remembered the mess in the living room.

"Oh dear!" she thought.

"What" her mother said, pronouncing each and every word as though it were a sentence, like she did when she was oh so angry. Her voice hissed like a boiling kettle.

"Are"

"You"

"Doing"

Devi could tell, even above all her confusion, it wasn't really a question Mom wanted an answer to.

"Oh," said Devi, lifting her palms to her mouth as reality hit her.

Above it all, she had completely forgotten to even pretend that she had gone to school.

Chapter 2

The Rasa Bhugola

Needless to say, when Devi's father came home that night, there was a lot of raising of voices that occurred. Devi had braced for it all to be directed at her, but halfway through, something miraculous occurred. The grown-ups in the room forgot she was there and began to yell at each other. Devi sat there watching them go back and forth and back and forth, and it suddenly occurred to her this was exactly like a Tom and Jerry cartoon – the one with the tennis match. And she didn't know what came over her, she couldn't help herself. She really tried not to, but then she let out a little giggle. It was a really tiny giggle, and she tried to stifle it quickly by covering her mouth and turn it into a cough, but it was too late. Her parents hit pause on the arguing to look at her, especially Mom, whose glare pierced her like a lance.

"That's enough from you. I don't know what nonsense you've been up to all day."

"Nonsense? You can clearly see she misses Ammamma. The child is grieving," Pa intervened.

Devi felt obliged at this stage to wear an expression that appeared aggrieved.

"Stop being so indulgent Sanjay, and constantly taking her side. It's because of all the coddling she's ended up this way to begin with."

"Neela, it's because my mother was here that you were able to go to work in the first place..."

"Or what, hunh, what exactly are you trying to say Sanjay? That my going to work is causing this?"

Suddenly, a small humming sound emerged and began to spread around the room. It was like a bee buzzing, a low drone, unmistakeable.

Her parents stopped arguing abruptly and looked at her again.

"What are you doing?" Mom asked.

"What's that sound you're making? Is it a tic? Since when does she have a tic?" Pa said.

"What sound?" Devi asked.

She couldn't hear any sound, just the shouting and now the silence.

"That moaning."

"Moaning?"

Mom looked a bit exasperated now.

Devi listened.

The 'Auuuuuuummm' was rising from her tummy, like the Voice / Ammamma / Butterfly had shown her. The sound was rising through her abdomen up to her chest now and threatening to erupt through her nose like shaken soda in a can. She closed her eyes and could feel it reverberate inside like a trapped echo bouncing off the cave walls. It felt cool and delicious, a whole nest of bees stirring inside a tree.

"Oh that?" Devi said, pressing her tummy and chest with her hands, wishing she knew how to make it stop now that it seemed to be activated. "I'm just hungry."

Pa looked at Mom and waved his hand in that exaggerated way as if to say, "you see." That got Mom quite riled up.

Mom began to open her mouth to say something quite sharp back to Pa, but she caught sight of Devi's face and quickly shut it. She would deal with that later.

She sighed. She would have to let this go for now. She would talk to Sanjay later. Devi hoped in a way that she wouldn't have to overhear from under her pillow.

Mom bent down to Devi and asked, in that voice that was extra sweet and completely disconnected from everything that had been said before, "Would you like to order some pizza and talk about Ammamma?"

Devi at first looked at her and wanted to ask, "Wait, is this a trap?" She didn't understand how she had managed to bunk school, make a mess, and still end up with pizza! She wished she knew the formula; she could sell it to other kids for money!

But perhaps it was best not to question this. She remembered Ammamma's words: 'why look a gift horse in the mouth?', she used to say. It was probably not the time to rile up Mom even more. In fact, if she took the offer gratefully, Pa would be obliged to one up and counter the offer with an even better offer. She looked into Mom's eyes and nodded with large grateful eyes.

Pa smiled, and quickly placed her favourite order, and, as Devi had guessed, over-ordered, with garlic bread, additional cheese dips – the ones he always said were too expensive – and a generous add-on of her favourite toppings, including pineapple chunks. He then began to tease her, "Make sure they are on your side of the pizza. Who puts fruit on pizza! Oh my gawd, how is that pizza?" until Devi forgot she was afraid and a little mad, and began to chase Pa around the living room.

While they waited for the delivery man to arrive, they cleaned up the house together, did the laundry, made her bed, wiped down the balcony door, and put the dishes to wash. Pa brought out a box of old photo albums from Ammamma's room, and he and Devi began to pore over them.

"Pa, do you remember the *vidukathai* Ammamma would tell?" Devi asked.

Pa wrinkled his brow to think, and suddenly broke into a smile.

"Oh yes!" Pa said. "All those mysterious one-liner riddles – she had a whole repertoire of them. It's been so many years since I thought of those, but maybe I could summon up a few."

"I was trying to remember some of them today but I couldn't," Devi said.

Her parents looked at each other.

"Does that make you feel sad?" Mom asked.

Devi nodded. Jokes and mischief apart, it was something that had been bothering Devi deeply.

"Pa, what if I forget her? In a few years, what if I forget what she looked like or the stories she used to tell me? I already can't remember all the riddles."

Tears rolled down Devi's cheek. She had tried so hard to remember today, and had realised there were so many parts of Ammamma she had already forgotten. She was feeling quite guilty.

Mom hugged her. "You won't forget her, okay. I promise. She's always going be a part of you. She's in how you think and how you speak and the things you do. She's always in your heart."

Devi nodded; it made her feel a little better. But really it was the butterfly she was thinking of. Ammamma was either here or had sent her. She wished she could tell her parents, but she knew, until she actually knew what was going on, it was just hers and Ammamma's secret, like so many they had shared.

Mom knew it was important for Devi to feel connected to Ammamma.

"We can organise these photographs of her into an album and make some of the dishes she used to like making. There are so many ways to remember her. Keeping her traditions alive is one. She used to love drawing the *kolam* at the doorstep every morning, right. Do you want to do that from tomorrow?" Mom asked.

Devi loved the idea. "Can I draw mine with chalk?"

"Yes, of course you can. We can do it together."

"And we can go pick flowers for pooja from the colony garden like she used to? Early in the morning?"

"Yes, of course, we can do that and put them on the altar. She would like that." Mom wasn't much of a tradition and altar person herself, and once Ammamma had passed, these little things she used to do around the house seemed to have passed too. Mom hadn't noticed or thought them very essential but she now understood why people kept some traditions alive; it was more a small way to remember the people who had passed them on, even if they didn't have any real belief or faith in the exact rite they performed. Lighting a candle and drawing a *kolam* was a small gesture by which they could remember Ammamma, and she was happy they could do something to keep her presence around.

Pa was thrilled. "Alright, come on then, let's have a weekly *vidukathai* night okay? Whoever scores the most answers gets the last slice of pizza. And you have to think up the best *vidukathais* for next week. No repetitions."

Devi raised her hand. "I'm going first."

"Shoot."

"A yellow canary swings high on a tree singing sour songs."

"That's it? You've got to give me more..."

Devi shook her hand and looked quite smug. "No, they're meant to be cryptic Pa. No clues."

"Give up? Give up?" she kept asking, as Pa gave her quite a few wrong answers, though she suspected he was doing it deliberately.

In the end, both Mom and Pa gave up.

"Elumicham pazham," Devi pronounced triumphantly, not even tripping over her tongue once. Ammamma had ensured she had said it many times.

Suddenly, it hit her. A lemon! Yellow! Lemon Yellow! That was it!

"Elumicham pazham!" she shouted.

Her parents looked bemused. What a funny little word!

Behind them, an electric buzz sizzled and flashed from Ammamma's now dark room. From where Devi was sitting, her parents opposite her, their backs to the corridor, Devi alone could see the wave of light emerge from the picture and cast a beam across the floor, its rays escaping from beneath the door to let her know, yup, that was it. She'd found the password!

The lemon, the answer was a lemon! Devi could barely contain her excitement. But for now, she would have to wait.

Mom and Pa clapped and Pa kept trying to say 'elumicham pazham' in silly ways with his tongue flopping this way and that until Devi was laughing till she cried.

"If you divide any word into three, you can say it easily," she said.

"Ohhh. Ammamma taught you that?"

Devi nodded, making Pa repeat after her "elumi"

"elumi"

"cham"

"cham"

"pazham"

"pazham"

"Now say it together."

"Supercalifragilisticexpialidocious."

"Nooooooooooo," Devi rolled over laughing.

"If you say my word, I'll say yours," said Pa.

And they spent the rest of the evening in silly speak.

Devi had another one.

"Mother sea, father sun. Who is it?"

They racked their brains for that one.

"Salt" came the answer.

Devi won the night and when she skipped off to bed triumphantly, her parents exchanged a high five.

"We should do this more often," Mom said. Pa just hugged her in return. The quarrel was forgotten. They were talking for a while, Devi could hear their murmurs as she drifted in and out of sleep.

"Mom?" Devi asked as her mother came in to switch off the light.

"Hmmm?"

"Do I have to go to school tomorrow?"

"Of course, you do. In fact, I think it's a good idea to have some classes for you to go to before and after school from now on. Will keep you busy and out of the house. You, young lady, are thinking too much. Alone in your head, with your memories is no good for you."

"Awww nooooo," Devi groaned.

"Awwwww yes! We'll discuss it in the morning. Goodnight, sleep tight!"

"Elumi-cham-pazham," Devi said, rolling the word around on her tongue.

"Such a funny word."

"It would make a good password, wouldn't it Mom?"

Her mother laughed.

"I guess so, nobody else would be able to guess it or spell it. Though if you got the spelling wrong, you'd spend a really long time trying to get into your own account."

"Goodnight Mom. Love you."

"Goodnight Devi-doo. Love you too."

Devi had wanted to see if the butterfly came back after her parents had gone to bed, but she had had an exciting day and was fast asleep before long.

In the morning, but of course, Devi was running a fever. Not a big fever, as she kept insisting, a baby teeny tiny one, just enough for her not to feel well enough to actually go to school. Mom checked her temperature and while the thermometer was in her mouth, patted her bed down like it was trying to enter the mall or something.

"Whaff ah fu fuing?" Devi said with the thing still in her mouth.

"Checking-for-onions-don't-speak-with-the-thermometer-in-your-mouth," said Mom, running all the words into each other really quickly as she made sure she got all the corners.

"Feckin fo fununs?" Devi asked, raising her hands and opening her eyes wide to gesture, "But why?"

"Fon fy fed?"

"Eh?" Mom said, pulling the thermometer out as it beeped its readiness.

"On my bed?" Devi asked, incredulous. "Why would there be onions on my bed?"

Her temperature was just above normal, 99.5, not enough to panic, but not normal enough to send her to school, her Mom thought. "Are you feeling ill?"

"Just a bit uncomfortable and headachy. Onions, Mom? Why onions?"

"Oh, didn't you know? You can raise your temperature by putting an onion under your armpit for a whole minute. Raise your arms, come on, let me smell..."

"Ewwww. Gross. NOOOOO, go away," Devi said, hugging her arms into a lock on her chest, utterly offended by the idea.

Mom laughed out loud. "Old hostel trick. Never mind, I don't think you're faking it, I just think you've been going through a lot and we hadn't noticed. Maybe you could do with a break?"

Devi nodded gleefully.

"Okay, so how does this sound? I'm going to queue up Moana on Netflix and put some hot chocolate in the micro."

"Oh god, the beeping! Not the beeping! Can't stand the beeping... anything but the beeping!"

Devi covered her face with her palm and groaned and moaned and flipped and flopped dramatically all over her comforter.

Mom laughed. "I was going to say I'll just put it in there and when you want it you can press the reheat button, okay?"

Devi nodded with relief.

"I'm also keeping some simple rasam rice and beans thoran and pickle in a bowl in the fridge. Same instructions."

"You'll make Ammamma's not-well rasam?"

"Yes, I'll make Ammamma's not-well rasam, the pepper garlic one, that should chase any fever out. Now you be good and no more than one show, okay? Don't be on your phone or on a screen all day either. Read a book, do some painting, sleep, nothing else. I'll try to leave work early today."

"OH NO NEED. Take your time. Not going anywhere. Am just going to be right here," Devi said, smiling a bit too broadly. Mom looked at her suspiciously.

Perhaps she suspected something was up.

"Are you up to something?" she asked.

Devi feigned innocence. "Who me? Nooooo. Whatever gave you that idea?"

"You do know that whatever it is I'll find out in the end, right? Moms know. Moms always know."

Devi thought of all the things Mom absolutely positively didn't know about and reckoned that she was probably safe. She shook her head. She couldn't give away anything by her expression.

"Not now, Devi, not now. Focus."

She simply had to get her parents out of the house to summon the butterfly again.

Devi's eyes flickered but she held Mom's gaze.

Mom suspected some impishness but she also knew Devi was in general what moms would describe as 'a good girl'. Her idea of mischief was to watch an extra episode of Glee or hide a bar of chocolate in her cupboard or to Google the answers to her math homework because she was feeling lazy. She didn't even go past the last speed bump let alone the colony gate when she went cycling. She wasn't the sort to go off on a bender and break the rules, or have mysterious friends over for a strange party when her parents weren't home. Was she?

Mom didn't blink.

"What?" Devi asked. "I haven't even done anything... *yet*"

"It's the *yet* I'm worried about..."

"Well, don't be. I promise you I won't leave the house."

"Or let anyone in?"

Devi hesitated. Well, technically she wasn't letting her, it, the Voice/ Ammamma/ the butterfly in, it just emerged on its own. She could give her word on that.

"Sure. Yeah. Nobody in. Got it." Devi spit on her hand like a pirate and stuck it out for a handshake.

"Ewwww. What is that, Devi! Go and wash your hand. Go at once."

Devi wiped it on her comforter instead while her mother groaned.

"Remind me to wash that in the evening."

"Nooooo, don't keep washing it, you'll take all the good smell out of it."

Mom sighed and sat down on the edge of her bed. Wait, what? Devi thought to herself, I thought I had fixed this. She is supposed to be moving in the opposite direction from me.

Mom, who would surely be late for work today, wanted to talk.

"Are you feeling okay honey? Is school difficult for you? Are you having a problem? Is that why you don't want to go? Your grades are falling, you're skipping days, not putting the effort into your homework projects..."

Devi considered the question thoughtfully. On the one hand, she could give her a straight answer and hurry this all up. Or, she could play along? Devi realised she was playing with fire here. If she said she absolutely hated school now, she might end up being taken out of a school that - truth be told - she didn't find so disastrously bad. Her teachers were quite kind and she was popular in her class. She didn't have any major problems as such. She better not create some for herself now. Should she say she was just feeling lazy? Oh dear, she might get hauled out of bed and marched to school any which way. Nope, better not risk it, she would have to play along.

"No Mom, I love school. I love my teachers and my friends. It's just, you know, Ammamma used to help me with a lot you know."

"I know. It's been hard for you..."

"Not just the food and snacks. She was *there... there* for *me*, you know. She chatted with me while I finished my homework. She helped me buy all the art supplies and put glitter on my projects. And I get that project marks and stuff matter to you, and it should, coz you're my parents, coz, you don't want a lazy duffer kid..."

Mom opened her mouth to say something but didn't want to interrupt her, nor did she want to say it was perfectly fine to be a lazy duffer kid, she'd have to think about that, so she shut it again.

"...but those things didn't matter to her. You know, Swati's mom always asks her friends her rank on the test when she comes to school for the pick-up."

"Really?"

"Yeah, and if you aren't in the top ten, you won't be invited to her next playdate or party or you can't even be in her group of friends. I just call her Swotty now. I can't even call Pooja on the phone because she's at tuition from 5-6, and then dance class from 6-7, and then dinner from 7-7.30, and then drama from 7.30-8.30, and then - can you believe it - she *has* to go for an evening aerobic-dance cycle-pilates class, like *has to* has to... And Neeta's mom is like '*beta*, which all classes have you joined?'"

Devi really got into the role now, doing the voices and everything. She rolled her eyes and flipped her hair and pushed back her non-existent glasses for effect. She didn't have a classmate called Pooja actually. But how would Mom know; there were 60 students in her class. Anyone could have been called Pooja.

"It's SO annoying. And Ammamma used to make up classes for me to attend with a straight face and then we'd both burst out laughing while the other parents searched for the class to sign up for it."

"Well Swati's mom isn't entirely wrong you know, the company you keep is going to define you, though I wouldn't be so harsh and upfront about it. And what's wrong with being productive and having a routine? Aren't there things you'd like to learn and do? We haven't forced you, but maybe a dance class, or a swim team... What about tennis coaching?"

"But I LIKE swimming all around the pool with my floaters. WHY do you want me to do 30 laps and hate it?"

"Because discipline and putting in the effort towards learning something is also a skill, right? And you should also have wins that make you proud of them, and yourself."

"Aaargh!! You sound just like them." Devi said, diving her head into her pillow again, groaning and moaning.

"It's okay, it's okay, nobody's forcing you to do things you don't want to do. Take your time and maybe we can come up with a list of things to join, maybe not as much as Pooja, but maybe one or two things every day and then something on the weekend. Maybe I should call Pooja's mom and see if there are classes you can go to together. Being occupied will be good for you, and keep your mind active. You rest now."

Devi was aghast. Talk about a plan backfiring. See? This was why she needed Ammamma. She slid under her bedcovers and pulled them over her head and stayed there until the sounds in the kitchen had faded and Pa had said goodbye from the living room and a little later, Mom.

The door clicked gently again. And all was as before.

The fridge hummed. The washing machine whirred. Somewhere in the building a pressure cooker went off and a doorbell rang. A clock ticked. The pav wala rang his cycle bell on the street below. And Laddu, the golden Labrador, barked at the pigeons in the balcony above theirs. Devi was alone again and she lay there listening to the passage of the day, forgetting for a moment why she had chosen to stay home in the first place.

"It's safe to come out now," the voice said.

Devi shot up out of her bed like a hot spring geyser out of a volcanic vent.

"Geez," she sighed, when her heart had stopped thumping. "You really need to stop doing that!"

"Psssst. Over here."

Devi leaned over the edge of her bed and hung upside down until she could see under it. An onion rolled out from under her pillow and disappeared into the dark corner.

"I can't see you," she whispered.

"Well of course you can't," the voice whispered back.

"You haven't said the password."

"Again?" Devi whispered back.

"Yes, again. It's a portal you know. It opens and shuts. Don't you know how portals work?"

Devi considered this information.

"Why are you whispering?"

"I don't know. It just seemed... um... appropriate," she whispered back.

"So you mean I will have to say this mantra thing every day?" Devi asked, groaning.

"Every time you'll want to open the portal, yes," the voice whispered back.

It struck Devi that she ought to get some clarifications before getting any further into this arrangement.

"But what is it a portal to? How do I know it isn't a portal to more homework?"

The voice sounded as though it were quite exasperated.

"Well, you won't know what's in the box until you open the box, right? And do you generally get your homework assignments through portals?"

Devi giggled. The upside-down conversation with no one in particular was making her quite light headed.

"Our teachers don't even use email properly. After you send them an email you have to meet them and ask them to check the email. They might never return to Earth if you opened them up to portals."

"Yes, well, chop chop. The email is the least of the wonders in the portal and you'll miss it if you don't hurry up."

Devi sat up on her bed and wiped her face with her palms like Ammamma had shown her. She looked into her palms and repeated the mantra.

"Auuuuuuuummmmmmmm"

The air in the room trembled in anticipation.

"Karagre vasate Lakshmi"

A gold light flashed onto her palm and hovered just above it.

"Karamule Saraswati"

A silver outline of a wing engraved itself on to the gold.

"Karamadhye sthitaha Gauri"

A rose-gold outline of the butterfly rose from the centre of her palms and filled in the details of the wings.

"Prabhate kara darshanam"

The butterfly shimmered into being and flapped its wings, lifting itself off her palm with a slight tickle and a nudge in its lift-off as it twirled around the room leaving a trail of stardust and sparkles.

This time Devi was not in the least bit frightened and she clapped her palms together and squealed with excitement, following the butterfly around the room as it went.

The butterfly flapped its wings lightly and descended to nestle on her shoulder.

Up close, Devi saw that each of its wings was as wide as the palm of her hand and shimmered iridescent gold, silver, and rose. Small lines, flecks and dots across its wing span created mystical patterns that appeared to fold into its contours like swirls of sugar balls on cupcakes. Its middle, like a long clothes peg, was a translucent mother of pearl, turning on the light as it caught it. As the butterfly fluttered its wings, the tinkling of tiny wind chimes emanated and drifted into the room. It shone like butter paper such that when Devi looked closely, she could see right through into the room beyond. It was almost like it was there, but also, wasn't, all at once, a fragile apparition that might as well disappear if you blinked twice into the sunlight.

Devi gasped, "Oh, you're beautiful!"

"Why thank you, Devi," said the butterfly, tittering shyly and setting off a small orchestra of melodies.

"Oh your voice is... different! You're not Ammamma?"

The butterfly shook its head sadly. "No, I'm sorry. I'm not. But I bring you her love."

"Then why did you sound like her? Did you change your voice to trick me?" Devi sounded a little offended.

The butterfly sighed. "No, no, I wouldn't do that to you. Truth is I am always the way I am. People hear me and see me according to what is most precious to them and what makes them feel most secure. They embody me according to what they love and that love, hidden or known, shapes how they hear me."

"So you look and sound different to everyone you mean?"

"Yes, I do."

"That's impossible. But then, there would be absolutely a thousand versions of you at the same time! To my neighbour Bunty you would have to appear as a talking peanut chocolate bar! I don't think he even loves his parents as much as he loves the bar."

The butterfly didn't laugh at the idea. She looked at Devi quite solemnly.

"You don't mean...?"

The butterfly nodded.

"A glowing celestial, great big one, I'm afraid."

"Wow. I don't even.... But that's really nice of you, you know, to show up in whatever form people wish for you in."

The butterfly shifted uncomfortably.

"People give me way too much credit for that you know. I am after all an expression of your own mind, so as I am seen, so I emerge."

"So, what I think of you as you have to be?"

The butterfly nodded. "Well sort of. I'm a fire butterfly, so whatever you think of with some flames around it."

"So, if I sat here and thought of you as a musth elephant would you turn into a musth elephant and run around the house destroying everything?"

The butterfly considered it. "A musth elephant with some flames around it, yes. No, I'm kidding. Well, it doesn't work that way you see. You have to truly at your core believe that

that is what I am, and that is what you believe in and that protects you, and you have to love that musth elephant as though it were an intrinsic part of yourself."

"Oooooh. So for you to be a musth elephant, I have to be a musth elephant first? Got it."

"More like, have a part of you that is a musth elephant. But otherwise, yup, summed up every religion in the world."

"So what is your name then? I suppose it can't be 'Ammamma'."

"I'm Hasya, I am mirth, laughter, joy."

"My mirth?" Devi asked, trying to scrunch up her forehead and remember the last time she had laughed a lot.

Hasya nodded. "Your mirth, joy in the world, in general."

"How odd, to be paid a visit by mirth. Where are the others? Why not raging fury or courage?" Devi asked, looking under the bed, half expecting to see the others there.

"Oh, we didn't want to crowd you; besides I am the messenger," Hasya said, tinkling to show off her wings. "Hence, the insignia. I'm normally just white."

Devi blinked at her. She wasn't joking. There were others?

"Oh yes, a whole nine of us. We are the Rasas."

"The Rasas?"

"Imagine you're watching a show and sometimes it makes you laugh but also makes you cry or feel afraid. Well, if the whole world was a show and you were watching it, then we, the Rasas, are how you feel. Without us, you wouldn't feel anything. It would be like watching a blank screen. Nothing would register."

"Oh yes, I know a boy in the school bus like that. Annoying fellow. Tell him a joke and he doesn't laugh. How much I've tried. He just never gets it," Devi said.

Hasya shifted testily. It felt like a personal failing sometimes.

"Sometimes people shut us out. It happens," she shrugged.

"Oh, I'm not saying it's your fault. Or maybe it is, just a little."

Hasya looked a little surprised.

"In what way, Devi?"

"I don't know. You keep saying you are a part of me, but I haven't felt particularly mirthful in a long while you know. Not inside. I laugh sometimes so Mom and Pa feel like I'm well, normal. Maybe you're not a part of me, or haven't been for a while. Maybe, you just don't show up for some of us."

"Oh, all nine of us are part of you, we are of everyone in equal measure; you just don't see us all the time. Some of us less and some of us more. Sometimes we stay hidden and everyone has their own favourites you know. And sometimes..."

The butterfly paused and stuttered.

"Sometimes...?" Devi encouraged her.

"Sometimes you lose sight of us and we have to remind you we are there."

"Oh, I know, it's kind of like when you're thinking of someone who is not there and then they suddenly call! Is that why you had to show up?"

Hasya nodded, "Sort of. Sometimes you need us to show up for you though you don't even know it."

"Ah, that's why people are suddenly giggling for no reason when they're angry or afraid," Devi exclaimed.

Hasya nodded, and flew around Devi's head in glee. She was so happy to be conjured up now by Devi, to be present and free.

"Let's go," Hasya said. "Follow me."

"Go? Go where?"

Hasya hovered in the air.

"Why, to the Rasa Bhugola of course!"

"The.. the.. what?"

"Home, to the World of the Rasas."

Devi followed Hasya to Ammamma's room.

"But how are we going?"

The butterfly pointed to the painting. Devi blinked at it.

"Put your finger on it and say the..."

Devi squealed. "Don't tell me, all I need is the password? I got this!"

Hasya nodded and flitted around excitedly.

"Go on, you know this one: 'a yellow canary swings high on a tree singing sour songs'. You set it yourself."

Devi's eyes widened with joy.

"Elumicham pazham!" she yelled out.

There was a woosh and swirl of bright yellow and what Devi thought must surely be the twittering of the canary, the air was filled with the gentle scent of freshly squeezed lemons, sour, pungent, but somehow, so clean and fresh. The world spun and Devi instinctively stuck her hands out and caught the side of the bed.

"No, no, let the bed go," Hasya squealed.

Too late.

The world spun faster and faster and back and forth, and Devi was just beginning to hope mightily that she wouldn't throw up, when it began to slow down. Suddenly, as though someone had hit the brakes, it stopped spinning and bounced hard on the ground. Devi and Hasya tumbled onto the slope on a hill so bright and cheerfully yellow, that Devi had to blink a couple of times to adjust her eyes to the light.

Hasya tumbled head-over-heels, as the inertia carried her spinning around, doing cartwheels through the air.

"Whoa whoa whoa," cried Devi as she bounced down the hillside.

"Phew, I never get used to that," Hasya said as she came to a halt the right way around. She turned around to find Devi, who was spinning like a wheel that had come off a car.

"Watch out!" cried Hasya as the bed – Ammamma's bed – suddenly appeared out of nowhere and landed just behind her, narrowly missing her head, and careened down the hill on a path of its own as they incredulously watched it go.

"Ammamma's bed!" cried Devi as she went head over heels, light as tumbleweed.

"I told you not to hold on to it!" Hasya shouted out.

"What will I tell Mom?" Devi hollered back, as they heard it go faster and faster and crash with a splash into a river at the bottom of the hill.

Devi, who was going faster and faster, put her hands down to steady herself and with a well-timed leap, jumped up onto her feet and launched into a steady run instead. She redirected herself with the momentum of her fall and ran towards the direction of the bed. Hasya got there first and was hovering over the crash site.

"Oh dear," Hasya said.

"Oh dear," Devi said, coming to a halt just next to Hasya.

The wreckage lay at their feet, a soggy, and a quite unrestorable bed, standing in the middle of a crisp clear flowing river.

"Well, that's that," said Hasya.

"Well, that's that," said Devi.

They looked at each other and burst out laughing. Feelings like guilt and worry didn't stick around Hasya. They all converted to mirth. They'd worry about it later. Mom wasn't here, right? Pfft. New worlds, new adventures, new problems.

"Hey, we're almost the same size here. Did I get smaller or did you get bigger?" Devi asked.

Hasya looked at herself and then at Devi, and shrugged.

"Does it matter? We're in proportion now. To each other and everything around us."

"Why is everything so yellow here? Even the grass is a deep shade of yellow."

"This is Adbhuta's land, the land of wonder, and she's also a fire butterfly. I guess that's why everything here is a burning brilliant yellow, and wonderful," Hasya explained.

The Earth was cheese. Devi knelt down and smelled it. Unmistakeably cheese. The pebbles were medallions of yellow, the sky was a bright Tuscan, and the sun beat down like a giant translucent glassy pineapple lollipop. The trees were citron, almost green, and their leaves mustardy. Around them the village had lemon brick walls and thatched roofs of dried-hay. Sunflowers bobbed about in the fields, nodding their heads to the breeze, and the fire-stone cobbled roads were edged with wildflowers, dandelions and buttercups. Bees buzzed and fat striped wasps drank in their nectar alongside sleepy oranges and orange emigrant butterflies; while the golden haze of air was filled with the song of yellow warblers, canaries, goldfinches, cardinals, and small yellow orioles. Only the stream babbling next to them, in which the bed now stood, looked outlandish in the otherwise banana countryside. It flowed a deep silver and blue.

Devi wished she had brought her sunglasses; she had to keep squinting at the brightness of it all. This is what it felt like to be so incredibly brilliant and shiny all the time.

"It's the colour you most associate wonder with," said Hasya, helpfully.

"Is this your world? The world of mirth?" Devi asked.

"It's my sister, Adbhuta's. It's the land of wonder. It is this colour because this is what wonder means to you in your mind."

"Because of Ammamma and the painting," Devi whispered to herself.

"Yes, but the painting is probably just a part of it," Hasya said, grabbing her by the hand. "Come on, let's go find Adbhuta. I'll introduce you."

Hasya and Devi joined the throng of people in the village market, every single one of them wearing butter yellow gumboots.

Hasya led the way to a stand in the farmer's market where they jostled for rubber ducky popsicles that dissolved in their mouths. They grabbed bowls of pineapple jelly and a handful of sugar syrup dried lemon wedges and stuffed them into their pockets. They sat by the honey fountain in the centre of the town to wait for Adbhuta, where they puckered their mouths at the alternating sour and sweet sensations of their bounty.

Devi inhaled deeply. The honey fountain flowed one moment deep rich gold and the other moment tinted with hues of peachy pink, its fragrance swinging.

"Apricot!" cried Devi, so loudly that a Hoopoe couple passing by stopped to stare at her.

"Oops," Devi giggled.

"Oops right back at you," said the couple, politely, thinking it was some sort of greeting in the land of the startling lady.

They seemed to recognise her. Devi was quite thrilled, having spent many hours trying to spot hoopoes during holidays in the mountains, after reading about them in *Haroun*

SCHO

and the Sea of Stories. A floofy Labrador out on his morning walk woofed at her in greeting, wagging his tail as he went. Ooh, was that Laddu from upstairs? A plump golden apple was out for a jog and she waved cheerfully at Devi too. A bus load of baby chickens dusted with colours went by, looking very much like the basketful she and Mom had bought off a vendor at the market to set free a couple of months ago. They chirped at her excitedly as they went off to school, tiny satchels slung across their shoulders. Everyone here was so friendly, so strange, and somehow, so very familiar.

A bunch of ducklings were playing in the fountain and would flap their wings in a great flutter every time Devi would correctly guess the flavour.

"Honeysuckle!" "Butter!" "Banana!" "Oranges!" she shouted out, and each time they went flapping about with great glee.

This was so much better than being at school. Everything here was so pretty and vibrant. Although everything in yellow seemed overkill, the more Devi hung around, the more it was growing on her. While she had first thought they were all many shades of one colour, the more she took it in, she realised that each one was ever so slightly distinct from the other, and no two shades were really the same.

A rustling sound rolled through the cloudless sky and Devi turned her face upwards to see what it was. It couldn't possibly be thunder, but perhaps they had planes here. The firmament seemed to tremble as though someone was taking off its cellophane wrapping. Glints and gleams of light seemed to be bouncing off it at multiple angles; the sky was turning like a yellow kaleidoscope. A large luminous Cloudless Sulphur butterfly came into view, her wings setting off a clinking, as of a tambourine, circling and swooping as she perched between Devi and Hasya.

Devi squealed with delight.

Hasya almost dropped her jelly in the honey fountain.

"Oh, Adbhuta! I told you not to startle us."

Adbhuta grinned and spread out her wings, every possible shade of yellow on them depending on which angle you looked at her from, to embrace Devi. She was taller than Hasya and though Hasya was all gold and silver and rose, and Devi had thought she couldn't possibly be prettier, somehow, Devi wondered if Adbhuta was. In quite a different way than her sister, being all one colour.

"Don't you dare think that. I can hear you," Hasya said, indignantly.

"Oops!" Devi said, covering her forehead with her hands and wishing she had tin foil to cover it up with.

"Can you all do that?" Devi asked.

"No, just her, because she's the messenger and that only works in the regular world. She's just trying to show off! Never mind her, I'm so glad you're here," said Adbhuta. When she released her from her embrace, Devi saw that her own arms and clothes were covered with a shiny pollen, speckling her orange and golden yellow. It was as though she had bathed in glitter.

Adbhuta was the source of all the glimmer in the world, and it was her job to keep the honey in the fountain constantly running. That hint of golden yellow was what fed the sense of wonder in anything, from a Labrador to a shiny new bicycle for a birthday or a goldfish or the Grand Canyon or a sunset on the beach. Devi couldn't take her eyes off Adbhuta. Who could? All who saw her were overcome by awe.

"I thought you were Miss Mirth and were only tickled pink by everything," Adbhuta said, turning to punch her sister. Hasya didn't really mind. She was not one to be jealous of her sister, besides she was used to it. Truth be told she found it quite funny, the way her humans went all 'aaaaaawwwwwwwwwweeeee' when they encountered Adbhuta. It also made her job a lot easier. Wonder flowed from mirth, and mirth from wonder, and Adbhuta and Hasya were like twins. Of the Rasa sisters, they had always been the closest. They teased each other a lot though.

"Ouch!" cried Hasya. She had just swallowed a spoonful of wobbly jelly and almost choked on it.

"There is a whole world of feeling, and reminder, I happen to feel a whole lot of them. Mirth is just my dominant emotion. The bees still sting, it's their nature to sting, you just happen to think it's wonderful when they do. Me? It hurts, but I laugh anyway."

"Just don't get stung in the land of my sister Raudra, the fury. It hurts so much and swells up all big and red!" Adbhuta said turning to Devi. Hasya made a face at her sister.

"Great. Scare our guest on the first day itself."

Devi didn't like the sound of Raudra at all. She didn't sound so nice. She hoped she would not be invited to her land, and if she was, would it be rude to refuse, she thought.

"Why is she so angry all the time?" Devi asked.

Adbhuta explained. "Did you know she's also a fire butterfly? All three of us, Hasya, myself and Raudra, we three are fire butterflies."

"Which means...?" urged Devi.

Adbhuta nodded. "Yes, the three of us are actually triplets, all born of the same fire energy. Mirth is as much fire as anger. Fire is the driving force behind us."

"But then how are you two so close and she so... so..."

"Isolated?" offered Hasya, looking away. "She did it to herself."

Devi looked at Adbhuta, not understanding. She had always wished she had sisters. It probably wouldn't feel so lonely then.

Adbhuta sighed.

"Raudra is a really nice person. She is the one who has always been the most fiercely protective of us. Problem is people used to call her hot-headed, angry, and constantly compare her to us."

"They called her the dark one, me the fair one, and Adbhuta the medium one," said Hasya.

As she grew up, Raudra began to believe that she was what people said she was – the bad one, the non-essential one, the one who didn't fit in. She believed that if that is what people called her, then they must be right and that is who she must be. So, she began to distance herself from us."

"But why you two? You didn't do anything to her."

"I guess it became a self-fulfilling prophecy. It made her angry to be constantly compared to us. And the more she was isolated and labelled, the angrier"

"and fiery-er"

"Raudra grew."

Devi felt sad for Raudra in that moment.

Fire was the most important discovery human beings had ever made. It's how people kept away wild animals and cooked their food. It could be a thing of great beauty as well. Mom loved her scented candles. The house looked so sparkly and pretty during Diwali. Yet, she knew it could burn down entire forests, and leave people homeless. Depending on what form it took, it could heal or harm. Devi looked around; she liked this sparkly yellow land of Adbhuta. A fire salamander scurried past with a taxi sign on its hat turned down to signal it was available for a ride and Devi looked on at it, amazed. Then she noticed the passenger hailing it.

"There he is! I knew it," squealed Devi, turning to clutch Hasya's wing as a yellow chameleon with a multi-coloured rf around his neck climbed into the cab and scooted past in e traffic. Soon, the chameleon was lost in the crowd.

"Did you see him? Did you see him?" asked Devi excitedly.

This time Hasya did drop her jelly, but thankfully not in the honey pond. She turned to see what Devi was saying. The jelly fell onto the honeycomb pavement, where it was quickly reabsorbed into the Earth. Good thing they didn't have to do much cleaning up here. The whole town was all self-cleaning. Since everything was a form of fire and organic, anything that fell down simply merged into the soil and within a few moments, returned to its original state. Hasya sadly watched her jelly merge into the ground.

"Oh listen," Devi said, suddenly realising why everything was yellow. "I remembered!"

"Ooooo, tell me," Hasya said. Now, she really couldn't wait to know.

"The last time we were all a great big family together was at my grandfather's house in Goa. It was one of those great big old-fashioned houses with tiled roof, and the courtyard in the middle with all the rooms around it."

"And it was yellow?"

It was but that wasn't the point alone. Devi shushed her.

"And there was a well and tall coconut trees outside. We never had to buy coconuts, we'd drink the water straight from the home ones, no straws and all. In the summers, all my cousins from so many extended sides of the family were there, it was like we were a hexadecadodecahedron."

Hasya and Adbhuta debated for a while about the possibility of such a shape and suggested gently to Devi that maybe that wasn't an actual one, but she was too excited to care.

If they were good, Appappan would take them to the beach where they'd buy all those sarongs with the messy prints and sunglasses from the shops that the foreigners bought their stuff from and play in the water. They'd eat a lot; there would be boxes and boxes of *chaklis* and *churmos* and *nevris* and *paatolyos* and *dodol* and *khatkhati*. When they played hide and seek there were just sooooo many places to hide that if you were the *kachcha nimbu* you would stay hidden and everyone would forget about you, were you not careful.

"And you were the *kacha nimbu*, so you were yellow?" Hasya asked, giggling.

Devi stopped to roll her eyes at Hasya for interrupting so many times, but also to catch her breath.

The painting was called Peeli Dhoop. It was painted by a really famous Indian artist, who had become Anil Appappan's friend, Maqbool Husain. The artist had come to Goa, which is where Anil Appappan and Ammamma, whose name was Julie before she had become an Ammamma, had lived throughout their lives. It was summer, the sun was blazing down, it was so hot there were vapours rising out of the tarred roads. The artist had been going from lodge to lodge looking for a place to stay. Appappan saw him in the market and felt sorry for him. Everyone had thought the artist was a bit mad looking, with long hair and he wore a long kurta and walked around without slippers. Problem was, so did everyone else. So no one wanted to give a man who didn't have shoes a room because they didn't believe he could pay the bill, even when he took the money out of his pocket and showed it to them. They thought he had stolen it. Also, in those days, Appappan said, everybody thought artists were no good fellows. But he knew they weren't all like that because Ammamma was an artist too. Ammamma was not a famous artist but she painted portraits so all kinds of wealthy people would come to see her for a sitting. People in those days didn't think it was a real job. Appappan, who was also a young man and knew what it was like to want to not wear shoes sometimes, brought Maqbool home and allowed him to stay in the house that he had just built. Though then it wasn't a big house, it was just a house, without all its verandas and extra rooms. Ammamma cooked for him and told him many stories, because she could also weave the most wonderful stories out of thin air, so really, it was Ammamma who had been the artist. The artist had such a nice time, he painted Peeli Dhoop for her as a thank you.

"I'll tell you a secret," Ammamma would whisper. And this was Devi's favourite part of the story though she had heard it so many times before. She would get all tingly and excited and begin to giggle.

Ammamma would lower her voice so nobody else could hear.

"Nobody knows, but the whole painting is the village, our village, in the hot blazing sun, and so many shades of it. And that house at the centre of it, is our house."

The house had gone, Appappan had gone, and now Ammamma had gone too. And Devi had believed for a while that meant the wonder had gone too.

Hasya nodded and sat quietly, just draping her right wing around her friend's shoulders. Adbhuta sat down on the other side of her and embraced her. A gentle electricity coursed through Devi as Hasya came into contact with her.

"Ooooh, what's that tingling?" Devi asked.

"That's just what mirth and wonder feel like when they begin to energise you again."

Adbhuta nodded towards Hasya.

"She's the girl who puts the linings on clouds you know. She can make anything seem okay."

Devi sat for a while and felt the buzz.

"It's like getting a phone recharged, right? Am I the phone?"

Hasya laughed, "Well, I've never had a phone so I don't know what it feels like to be one, but I guess you could say that."

Devi was wrong. The painting hadn't disappeared. Here it was, a whole vibrant, living land, deep inside the Rasa Bhugola. Every contour lit up pulsing with a yellow light, and all she had to do was close her eyes and see the painting in her mind's eye, the way Ammamma had taught her.

Here, in the village of the Peeli Dhoop, everything seemed just another shade of yellow. And when everything was just another shade of the same thing, Devi thought, that meant everything could become a big bright yellow again, even if it seemed like it was just pale, faded, almost-white for now.

"Yellow is always yellow, right?" Devi said, feeling a little more cheerful.

Adbhuta nodded. "Yes it is."

There was always enough yellow in anything if you looked hard enough. You just had to add a bit of this and a bit of that and you could make anything yellow again.

Devi felt much happier. The sky was filling with puffy lemon cotton candy clouds now and they swung about this way and that, casting candy stripe patterns on the ground. It was pretty awesome.

Sometimes, we take the simple but beautiful things in our lives for granted. Clouds with all their weird and funny shapes, constantly changing and drifting, moving across continents and seas as they pleased, without boundaries or passports, were so cool, thought Devi. She remembered lying on her back in the grass and watching them pass by for hours. Perhaps, she thought, not having the time or the space to gaze upon such things – the things that filled us with wonder – was both a good thing and a bad thing.

"How so?" Hasya asked.

"The more we see things, we lose our sense of wonder about them, we only seem to recognise it as wonder when it's rare. Like, for instance, I drew a *kolam* today and I thought it was pretty special and so did my neighbour aunty. I guess if I drew one every day, people would just think it's a normal thing and stop complimenting me for it," Devi said. "And I like the compliments."

"See, she gets it," exclaimed Adbhuta, nudging Hasya.

"Also, you'll admit that if people went around gasping in wonder at everything all the time, it would be pretty odd. And annoying!"

Hasya started giggling and Adbhuta glared at her.

"Like we can't be going 'wow lemon', 'wow flower', 'wow bus', 'wow Pa came home', 'wow this milkshake', 'wow this door unlocked', all the time," Devi teased, seeing Adbhuta getting huffier and puffier.

Hasya chimed in, "or 'wow butterfly', 'wow bird', 'wow cloud'," she said, pointing upwards.

Devi looked up and noticed a great churn in the sky. The wind, clouds and space were twisting and turning now, the light dappling the roads and buildings. As the shadows got deeper and darker, all of it began to be stained the gamboge of a monk's robe. All in the market square around them began to look up and pull out their umbrellas. Some gathered their shopping bags and the sprightlier ones began to make a dash home or to the nearest shelter.

"What's happening Adbhuta? Why are people leaving?" Devi asked.

Hasya looked at Adbhuta, her face a little flustered, her forehead wrinkling into fine frown lines.

"It's just... it must be raining over the mountains and sometimes the rain can pelt down quite... how do I say it... hot."

"Hot? How?" Devi raised an eyebrow.

Adbhuta sighed. "That's my fault. I thought it would be fun to have lemon candy rain but I didn't realise sugar can only pour when it's..."

"Really really hot!" Devi squealed as a large sticky droplet fell on her arm.

"Yes, and when it's cold, it's hard and it's like being pelted with stones."

"Ouch ouch ouch!" Devi hopped about now.

"Adbhuta you really need to fix this." Hasya frowned at her. "Come on, let's go Devi. We also have to restore the bed before your parents get back," reminded Hasya.

Devi leapt up with alarm, forgetting the downpour of molten sugar.

"Oh gosh, yes, ouch, we have to leave or Mom, ouch, will absolutely cook me for dinner!"

"Hush now," soothed Hasya. "You don't worry about it."

Hasya held out her wings and held both of Devi's hands in her own. She began to flutter her wings ever so slightly, activating a gentle breeze of sparkles and shimmers that formed a protective orb around them. Devi could feel her feet rise off the ground and before she knew it, she too was moving upwards, higher and higher, above the sugar-leaking clouds, until the tawny landscape beneath her began to look like the pages of an old much-loved book – all the beings on it like letters – getting scrawnier as they rose above them. Devi looked up and, in the distance, she saw the gamboge emanating from the heart of a darkness approaching the mountains, not at all swift and airy as monsoon clouds often were, but menacing, like a spreading stain. The more Devi looked at it, the more it seemed to suck her in. For a moment, Devi felt a surge of fear well up within her. No sooner did this arise, than her feet turned to lead and she began to plummet through the sky like a dropping pebble, tugging Hasya down with her.

"No no no no no no no," squealed Hasya, pulling at Devi with all her strength. "This – a – way unh argh eee," Hasya grunted, tugging the other way.

But Devi was getting heavier and heavier.

"Don't look there, look at me, LOOK AT ME," Hasya was shouting by now, which if you have ever heard wind chimes, you'll know is very hard for someone with a voice like that to do. Adbhuta, who was watching from below, saw them plummet and raced upwards like a bolt of lightning, and caught Devi around the waist. Adbhuta's flash was blinding enough to momentarily dislodge the grip of darkness from Devi's eyes.

Devi shook her head and blinked, pulling her gaze away from the mesmerising cloud. Adbhuta grabbed her face and turned it towards her. The sisters were looking very relieved.

"What just happened?" Devi asked, alarmed.

Hasya was back to her shining and bright self, her face beaming through a thousand laugh lines and her wings enveloped Devi in starlight. In such a haze of delight, Devi couldn't help but smile. Instantly, Hasya felt the weight release and they flew up again.

"Tell me another one," said Hasya, completely ignoring what had just happened, and not taking her eyes off Devi's.

"Another what?" said Devi.

"*Vidukathai.*"

"Now?"

"Oh yes please, I love hearing them. I'd love to hear a few before you return home."

Devi shrugged and, forgetting she was quite high above the firmness of Earth right now, began to tap her forehead to think of one.

"Oh yes, I have one: No hands, no feet, still I keep running, who am I?"

They had begun to whirl faster and faster.

Hasya had to shout above the sound of the spinning to be heard: "Water?"

Devi shook her head.

"Tiiiiiiiiimeeeeee," she shouted as they spun out of Adbhuta's land, and lost sight of each other. The yellow land of wonder, and the whole of the Rasa Bhugola, disappeared in a blur.

As she opened her eyes, Devi's mother was standing over her head feeling her forehead.

"Hey ducky, have you been asleep all day? Must have dozed off in Ammamma's room while reading," she said, bending to the floor and picking up her well-worn copy of *The Secret Garden*, and placing it neatly on her nightstand.

"Mom?" exclaimed Devi, her head still spinning a little from the flight.

Devi sat up in a panic and felt for Ammamma's bed, patting at it to make sure it was there. A wave of relief gushed over her as she realised she was sleeping on it. It was there, all firm and soft and cosy and intact, just as Mom had left it.

She rubbed her eyes and looked at Mom, who had started laughing.

"Quite lost in a dream, were you? Come to the kitchen, I'll make you some hot chocolate." She turned and began to head down the corridor.

"Coming!" Devi called out.

As Devi swung her feet over, she landed in a puddle of water that she could swear, okay maybe she just hoped, wasn't there a moment ago when Mom was standing just there. She bent down to feel the underbelly of the bed. Oh dear! It was quite damp. And as she stuck her hand in her pocket, she found a handful of small yellow lemon shaped boiled sweets, no larger than her pinkie fingernail, that still managed to mightily pucker her whole face when she tossed them on her tongue.

Chapter 3

The Chase of Darkness

Devi grabbed a slice of chocolate cake from the fridge (there was *always* cake in the fridge), and pulled a chair to climb onto the kitchen counter, so she could sit on it cross-legged and eat it with her fingers. Mom watched with amusement and said nothing. Well, in truth, Mom couldn't have gotten a word even if she had tried. Devi was full of chatter and banter. Of course (but *of course*) she couldn't possibly, *possibly* tell Mom what was really happening, so she was kind of over compensating by filling Mom in with all the *other* details of her day, the kind of news that Mom usually asked for and Devi typically replied to with "meh, nothing much" and a shrug. Mom just attributed it to the after-effects of a good rest and a lonely alone day. As Mom prepped for dinner, Devi brought out her entire storehouse of happenings at school, all the gossip, the crises her friends were facing, all the memories of Anil Appappan, and the many, many memories of Ammamma and the Goa house. It was as though a frozen fountain of happy times had thawed in the sunlight and begun to flow. When Pa came home, he opened the door with his key and stood there for a moment, in surprise. He exchanged glances with Mom, who just gently shrugged and shook her head, pursing her lips as if to say "don't ask me."

Clearly, her parents thought, Devi was on the mend and the time off from school was doing her good. Mom, secretly worried, had called up a counsellor a friend from her workplace had recommended that morning, to have a chat.

"It's okay, sometimes we all don't feel like going to school or work. We don't want to fit into the rigid routines of our day and rush between twenty classes. It's perfectly normal to want to sleep it out, or just do nothing for a while. What's important is the ability to express it, to have avenues to talk about how one is feeling," the counsellor, a compassionate sounding lady, had said. Well, thought Mom now to herself, the avenues are clearly there and she's running down them. That did assuage some of her concerns.

Mom had expressed her doubts about this strategy to the counsellor though. "Yes, but expressing one's feelings doesn't pass exams, or get us into good colleges, or win us awards, or help us earn money, right?" she argued.

The counsellor lady considered what she was saying and had replied: "Neither does having a break down when you've been pushed so hard to do everything you don't want to do that you absolutely can't bear to move a step further."

Mom didn't have any questions after that. She still was a bit concerned about Devi, but she saw that it was as important to feel motivated as it was to be good at things. One was clearly of no use without the other.

"Besides," the counsellor had said, "when she feels genuinely free and light inside, the number of things she is good at might increase exponentially or change, though not always in the direction you expect them to. So be open to her flights of fancy. That's her imagination setting itself free."

Mom was explaining all of this to Pa, over a drink in the living room, long after Devi had gone to bed. Before that though, Devi had made Pa get a stool and stand on it to open the top row of cupboards in what was now the guest room, the one that nobody ever stayed in, to retrieve all of Ammamma's paintings, some of the lovely portraits and landscapes she'd done. They had been carefully wrapped in newspaper and put away and out of sight. They had been a bit hard to look at.

"Now?" Pa had asked, looking tired.

"Now," Devi had said, her hands on her hips.

"You might change your mind in the morning," Pa protested, not really wanting to pull things down and put them up and stand on stools and all of that.

"Well then, you'll just have to climb right back up again won't ya, Pa?" Devi shot back. "Getting too chubby are we to do that twice?"

"I'm telling Ammamma in my mind how difficult you're being," Pa said, pretend grumbling.

"You do that. I already told her about you," Devi retorted.

Pa realised he wouldn't win this one, and besides, he had liked the paintings too. He had liked Peeli Dhoop too, and thought about it often. It was the kind that stayed with you. So, he took the stool out of the balcony, careful to switch off the fan first so its blades wouldn't hit him on the head, and retrieved the paintings out of their hidey hole.

Pa was secretly glad, because Devi had been the darling of his parents, and the more Devi began to speak of her memories of them, he realised that he had missed them too. Because Pas aren't really supposed to cry but be the strong heads of the family, he had been trying to show that he was back to normal, and getting on with his work, when in fact, he was carrying his grief like a packed lunch with him everywhere he went.

Every day, Pa tried a little more to be like his Pa, and remembered that when his Amma was around, the nicest thing she would say to him was, "you're just like your father, he would have been so proud of you." He had begun to spend longer and longer hours at work, and had pushed away any thoughts of his parents every time they came up. They came up anyway, like when someone brought Diwali sweets and he remembered that his mother's *karanjis* were so much better. He thought it best not to say such things out loud. When Devi asked, "will I forget her?" he realised he had the same questions too, just he hadn't said them out loud to anyone until then, not even to himself. So, the thoughts Devi was mulling over were helping him think about it all too. Along with the painting, he had brought down a small black and white photo of his parents taken just after they had first gotten married. Amma was looking shy and Appa was stiff and tall, the way they were while posing for photos in the old days. And behind them was the mango grove and the old house. They looked happy. Pa slipped it into his wallet. If you pushed down the memories of people you loved and who had hurt you in one way or another, maybe by arguing with you, or moving away or dying, and you felt abandoned, then maybe the hurt stayed with you long after the picture of them in your mind was gone. Maybe that was their way of lingering. When you put them together and gave them a shape, they didn't have to linger in other ways. They had a place to be with you. It was nice to be able to remember his parents now, a little more openly, a little more in stories and memories and traditions, in this way. Mom stretched a hand out and squeezed Pa's.

"Sometimes," Mom said to him, "we forget in the rut and routine of everyday living, that we're not just Mom and Pa, but people too, Neela and Sanjay, sons and daughters, children to parents we have loved too."

A tear rolled down Pa's cheek, and he quickly wiped it away.

"I guess we owe Devi some thanks," Pa said.

"For her silly *vidukathais* and all! By the way have you prepared any for this week? She's going to beat us hollow you know."

And they forgot what they'd been sad about and began to quickly Google riddles on their mobile phones.

In the corner, beneath Devi's bed, Hasya smiled and the soft tinkling of wind chimes gently rang through the house with the breeze.

Devi woke up early the next day and crossed her legs on her bed. When Mom peeped in, she saw her looking into her palms, folded in front of her hands, about to say her prayers.

"What are you doing?" asked Mom, almost falling to the floor in shock.

Devi looked up at her, her eyes bright with purpose, and smiled serenely.

"Oh, I'm saying my prayer."

"Your prayer?" Mom was looking at Devi like she had never met her before.

"The one Ammamma taught me to say in the mornings. You know..." Devi winked at Mom conspiratorially, "as part of our thing of remembering her through traditions."

Realisation replaced Mom's confused expression and she nodded. In truth, she had completely forgotten about all of that. She wondered how long this phase would last. She'd better go get the design for the *kolam* set up in the meantime. To Devi, she said,

"Wonderful! When you finish, you can come help me draw a *kolam* outside the door."

"Be there in a moment," Devi chirped.

She quickly recited her shloka.

"Auuuuuuum

Karagre vasate Lakshmi

Karamule Saraswati

Karamadhye Sthitaha Gauri

Prabhate kara darshanam"

Nothing happened. Devi looked around expectantly. There was no flash and tinkle and chime and glimmer and glint. All was just as before.

"Psst. Over here," Hasya's tinkling voice came.

Devi swung her head under her bed. There Hasya was, a pinpoint of light in the corner, like a soft glow bug in the forest.

"Whatchyoudoingthere?" Devi exclaimed, befuddled. "Where's all your paraphernalia of stars and lights and shimmer and shine and stardust and galaxy food today?"

Hasya shrugged and whispered. "You know. Grown-ups. Why'd you summon me when they're around?"

Devi laughed. "They're not so bad you know. They don't eat butterflies for breakfast."

Hasya shuddered. "Don't joke. You don't know some of the ones I've seen. They're like musth elephants in the morning."

"You don't like musth elephants, do you?"

"No, I don't. They're Raudra's favourites," said Hasya, as a shiver went through her. Problem was, every time Hasya shuddered, she tinkled too. So it looked really odd to Devi, that happy sound coming from such an aversion.

Devi thought they'd have to have a talk about this sister one of these days. For now, she had to go. Mom was expecting her at the door in a moment.

Devi whispered urgently at Hasya.

"I had to let you know I can't come today. I have to go to school. I want to though, it's just... I can't have an excuse every single day."

"Oh, sure you can. You'll be back before they know you're gone."

"But school?"

"You remember. The world is a show?"

Devi nodded.

"Well, you can just hit pause. In Rasa Bhugola, time doesn't run. You can be stuck in a Rasa for as long as you choose. The whole world can have moved on but if you're stuck in joy, there you are, and if you're stuck in grief, well there you are. Point being, I can bring you back before school begins. If you want to, it's up to you really."

Devi was doubtful about this.

"Are you sure?"

Hasya winked and sparkled. "Didn't you get Ammamma's bed back? A bit creaky and damp I agree, but on the whole, you didn't get into trouble, right?"

Devi nodded, which was an odd thing to do while hanging upside down, because you have to nod upwards, which is more difficult than nodding downwards. Although if you mulled over it, Devi thought, when you nod your head goes both ways, upwards and downwards, so there shouldn't be any real difference. Devi was instantly lost in pondering the intricacies of nodding upside down.

"What now?" called Mom again, at the door, hurriedly. She would be late for work. "Come on!" Devi swooped upwards, her ponytail flying as it went and the edge of it smacking her in her eye. That's why you don't nod upwards. Got it.

"Ouch! Coming! Just dropped my... er scrunchy..."

She grabbed a couple of coloured chalks from her dresser and skipped along the corridor behind her. Mom had already laid out the dots for her for a simple flower design with eight wide petals that Ammamma used to do variations of every day.

"Ooh, I know how to do this one," Devi squealed. She had seen Ammamma do it so many times. "Easy peasy," she said. Yet somehow, when she began, she missed a dot here and a dot there and ended up drawing some pretty alien looking flower. Mom had to crane her neck to figure it out, but as a first attempt, it was "not bad" Mom said.

As much as Devi was excited by the prospect of travelling to distant worlds, for now, she was lost in her own, as she carefully coloured each petal a different colour. She may have made it too big though because when Pa was leaving for office, he had to do the whole tippy toe thing around the edges so as not to mess it up. And he was not a man who was light on his feet, so tippy toeing was his contribution and sacrifice to the process, he said. Devi threw her head back and laughed and laughed at that because he made it sound like the hardest thing he would have to do all day, which was kinda not true. Devi had peeped at his laptop screen when he was working once, and he had so many numbers on it, she had to ask him "where are all the sentences?" and then he had laughed and laughed too. That stuff looked pretty hard to Devi. She made a mental note to ask Pa how his day went in the evening when he got home from work.

Suddenly, an idea struck her and she ran back to her room to get the craft supplies box out from her drawer. From a messy entanglement of ribbons, sketch pens, shoe laces and allied craft supplies, Devi pulled out a little squeezy tube of silver glitter. Scampering back, she carefully outlined her flower in silver and stood there admiring it.

"There," she said, "glitter makes anything look pretty." The milk man came by just then and rang the neighbour aunty's doorbell. When the neighbour aunty opened her door, they both stood there admiring her handiwork telling her how wonderfully bright and cheerful her flower was.

"I see traces of Ammamma in you, girl," the neighbour aunty, who was somebody's Ammamma too, said.

Devi did a snap and point with her fingers back at the neighbour Ammamma aunty. "Yup, and that part of me is all glitter."

"Ammamma would be so proud," the neighbour Ammamma aunty said. And Devi thoroughly agreed.

Feeling quite satisfied with herself, Devi skipped back to the bathroom, had her wash, changed into her uniform, requested Mom to redo her ponytail and had her breakfast. She was all dressed and prepped and ready by 8 am, which was even sooner than Mom was ready for work.

"You're bright and early this morning," Mom said to her, "would you like me to drop you to school on my way?"

"Ohhhhh NOOOOOO," Devi said, a tad bit too vehemently.

Mom raised an eyebrow.

Oh no, Devi thought, she'd totally ruin her chances of going back to the Rasa Bhugola today if she didn't cover up this hole in her cover up.

"Homework!" she exclaimed. "I asked Pooja to WhatsApp me the class notes I've missed, so I have to sit and copy everything now or Miss will be really mad. Gotta go," she said, skipping off to her room before Mom had a chance to question her on the details.

Devi carefully shut the door and got on her hands and knees and peeped under her bed. There Hasya was, a soft glow-worm light, dimmed and gentle, glowing in the corner.

"What if a spider got you?"

Hasya laughed. "It would just laugh and laugh until its belly shook and its sticky web would come apart."

"Wow you really wield laughter like a weapon, don't you?"

Hasya alighted on her finger and shook out her wings, still muted but quite spectacular none the less. “Let’s go find Peeli Dhoop and say the password and puhleeez, this time ...”

“...don’t hold the bed. Got it!” Devi said, winking.

Devi waited for Hasya to flutter on to her hand. Then, she slipped into Ammamma’s room, and stood in front of the painting. How strange Devi thought, this time it looked like it was all a shade of green. Was she seeing things? But there was no time. She had to get out of there before Mom asked to see her homework. She inhaled and pronounced the password.

“Elumicham pazham!” she said.

And they were off, tumbling through space like dandelion seeds in a hurricane.

“Whoa whoa whoa whoa whoa,” Hasya said as she went.

Devi went with a more all-over-the-place “yeaaaahhhhhhhwaaaaaaghhhhhhhaaaaaaaaaa...” sound.

This time, Devi found herself wooshing down the silvery blue river on the back of a giant turtle, who tipped her a salute and turned his meter down as she tumbled on board. She thought it best to sit down cross legged on his back and wear the seat belt he kindly nodded towards. The turtle taxis started out gently enough but Devi soon realised they were careening down vigorous rapids. She hoped there wasn’t a waterfall coming. She’d seen that in the movies; there was always a gigantic waterfall at the end of these things. She clutched the edges of the broad shell and braced for it. The river flowed faster and faster, white tips flew up as the waters crashed against large boulders and the turtle taxi took the corners like a Formula 1 driver. Devi knew turtles were pretty slow-moving creatures, but in the white water, clearly, turtle taxi guy had no speed limit. Perhaps, turtles were only slow at the things people forced them to do, and when they found what they really got a kick out of, they just went for it.

The river's banks were edged by a verdant and dense rainforest, flanked by giant red cedars, teaks and rubber trees whose canopy formed a light green umbrella over their heads. As Devi hurtled along the river's path, she noticed the forest wasn't empty. There were small animals approaching the riverbank to cheer her as she went along. She might have been a little more alarmed at the whole situation if it wasn't for them. They seemed, somehow, so familiar, as though she had met them all before. She looked closely. Then she gasped. She had. She had met them all before. On the river banks stood all the love Devi had ever received. There were her parents and her grandparents and aunts and uncles and cousins. There were her friends. There was the puppy she had fostered when she'd found it in a cardboard box near the colony gate. There were the kittens from school. The parrots who came to her window for fruit and grain. There were horses she had petted on holidays in the hills and stray dogs and donkeys whom she had fed sugar lumps to. Even the sparrows who pecked at seed from the bird feeder. Splashes of water doused her completely and she caught her breath but instead of feeling wet and cold, she began to feel warm and nurturing all over her. She gasped. This was what it felt like to be surrounded by love on all sides she thought, positively drenched in it. Every time she felt a great wave of love surging inside her, the river doused her some more and while it left her whooping, she didn't mind so much. Where the river was most energetic, the forest was most dense and vibrant, its foresty insect sounds, bird hoots and calls, stronger and louder than the crash of the waters. No matter how loud the rapids got, these voices of all those Devi had ever loved and who had loved her back rang louder. After all, as Ammamma used to say, it was the feeling of being supported and connected that made beings want to grow tall and strong and be their best. The urge to flourish was rooted in love, and the love the Earth wore – green, vibrant and flourishing – was its ornament and its beauty.

As they arrived in the central dock in the land of Sringara, it occurred to Devi that this was what Earth would have seemed like once, when it was still pristine: lush, everything abundant and fertile. The turtle taxi pulled up to the riverbank landing. Hasya flew off hers and Devi leaped off hers, remembering to turn around and give the turtle a hug. Adbhuta had been waiting for them there, her yellow wings acquiring an emerald tint in the green light, filtered through the rainforest canopy. As Devi stepped onto the land, she discovered it was a soft moss, and her foot sank deep into its spongy fullness until she couldn't see her feet anymore. Delighted, she threw off her shoes and squished her toes down into the living carpet. It was the softest thing she had ever felt, like standing in cake icing. Grasshoppers and speckled ladybugs leaped up and jumped out of her way as she walked. She was shocked to realise that when she wore her shoes and wasn't paying as much attention to the ground, she probably couldn't see or feel these tinier insects that also shared the land. Perhaps she had inadvertently stamped on some of them without even knowing it. The grasshoppers called her name now as they leaped up. "Hi Devi," "Hello there Devi," "Welcome Devi," "Watch out there Devi," and as she waved and blew kisses at them, she felt deeply regretful and apologetic. She must have seemed like a jolly green giant to the insects in the grass.

The trees around her were of all kinds, tall coniferous, evergreens and deciduous, tropical and arctic all at once. The land was the world's biggest tree nursery. There were even Christmas trees and mango trees with ripening fruit on them, right next to each other. All seasons in Sringara were the season of growth.

"Sringara is a water butterfly, and water being the basis for life, it contains the urge to manifest," Hasya explained. "All that is ready to germinate originates here and spreads through the world." Love was the green thriving heart of the world, filled with the desire to self-propagate. Everything in the land of Sringara was moist with potency.

"But isn't fire the enemy of water?" Devi asked. "How does that work? How do the two of you work together?"

Hasya laughed. "Well technically, we are butterflies, not actual fire and water. But yes, the three of us fire Rasas

– mirth, wonder, and anger – are tempered by water. Which means if we get too much, cross boundaries, forget ourselves, we are brought down to Earth by Sringara, Vira, Karunya and Vibhatsa – the four water butterflies. So, we each work together but we also contain and restrain each other."

"I get it," Devi said, "you're like each other's monitors."

"You here for me?" a cheerful voice said.

It was Chakresh, the nursery manager, who also happened to be a chameleon. He had been walking around in a multi-coloured scarf around his neck, with a pair of pruning shears in his hand. He went round and round all day and he never got dizzy doing it or had to sit down. It was his job to run up and down the trees to check if they were doing okay, had any diseased or rotting bits, and take away what had shrivelled up so the young and healthy saplings could grow unencumbered. He was passing by a zigzag tree, which was the interlinking messenger tree between the others, when he spotted Devi and Hasya chatting, and stopped to say hello.

"THE CHAMELEON WITH THE SCARF! THERE YOU ARE!" Devi cried, screechily loud, right in Hasya's ear.

The chameleon looked her down and up and up and down and nodded frantically.

"You've been visiting a lot recently. About time," he said cheerfully. "And it's Chaki, pleased to meet you."

"What a pretty scarf you have there, Chaki," Hasya said.

"Thank you. Knitted it myself. Isn't the weather just a bit chilly here today?"

Devi found herself nodding back at him vigorously, it seemed a bit contagious a habit. It invariably startled her that all the beings here already seemed to know her while she didn't seem to know them at all. It occurred to her that Chaki was all green. How had he spotted her in Adbhuta's yellow land? And he hadn't been any colour in particular on the balcony.

"He's a *rangrupiya*," Hasya whispered back.

Devi looked confused.

Adbhuta explained. "*Rangrupiyas* are colour shifters. The chameleons are the only ones who travel freely between one land and other," Hasya explained. If everyone else did go around as much as Chaki did, there would just be great confusion. Was something angry or was it wonderful? So all the beings of the Rasa Bhugola pretty much stuck to the lands they were born in.

"But don't some things belong to more than one Rasa Hasya? Somethings that you love can also make you mirthful. But they also make you sad sometimes," Devi asked.

"We all have a bit of all the Rasas in us Devi. We all have a tinge of sadness, a smidgen of love, a bit of anger, a dollop of wonder.... That's how it goes. It's just in each land, one emotion is dominant."

"Ahhh, got it. You must have seen wonderful things on your travels Chaki," Devi said, turning back to their new friend.

The chameleon tree gardener looked her up and down. Then he paused and shook his head. "I've seen some beautiful things here, and also some things you don't want to see," he said.

Chaki looked so sad Devi wanted to hug him, but was afraid he might think her a bit forward, since they had just met. So, she asked him about the things he loved the most instead – his trees. "How are all your trees doing, Chaki?"

Chaki looked pleased. He loved talking about his trees. He'd grown them all up since they were babies and knew them all by name and personality. Few people realised that trees were people too, with unique characteristics and were quite friendly. Most people thought they all just looked alike, which was quite rude to them. Even the trees that were from the same families had different names and life stories. They loved to be hugged for instance. They whispered, they made friends, they even shared secrets by hands underground and by passing messages between themselves. The frill on Chaki's neck stood up as he bristled with pride. "I've been looking after some of these babies since the dinosaurs," he said. It occurred to Devi that meant he had been around for quite a while. "But these days I'm not able to save some of them. The ones in Shanta's land are gone I'm afraid. I'm not able to reach them. Some of the oldest trees in the world, completely destroyed by a raging forest fire, one wants to weep. Two sectors are dying with the disease. Trees that have been healthy for years are turning black overnight and dropping to the ground, crumbling like dust."

"Disease? Oh that's terrible. Do you know what the disease is? Is there any cure?" Devi asked.

Chaki shook his head sadly.

"It's greed little one," he said. "It's taking over everything. They need to find a cure before it's all gone."

Devi was alarmed and lost her balance, reaching out to clutch a hanging vine to steady herself. It turned out to be a green tree snake, perfectly harmless, that she tugged on. She screamed nonetheless when she saw it open its mouth and recoil.

"Ouuuuuch," the tree snake hissed, really annoyed at being so rudely awoken when she was just minding her own business and was fast asleep.

"You woke me and now you're sssssssssscreaming? Nicccccccccccccccee."

"Oh, I'm so sorry," Devi said to the snake.

It hissed-grumbled at her and moved to a different spot, one that she couldn't reach, and went right back to sleep.

Chaki nodded at the snake. "That's Hissto. Their lot sleep hanging upside down. They haven't had much sleep lately because all the spots have been taken over by their cousins fleeing from the other lands. The trees are getting crowded now. There's limited resources and fewer spots."

"And so many refugees," Hasya chimed in.

"Is that where Sringara is?" Devi asked.

Hasya nodded. Sringara was off looking after the stream of the displaced coming in over the borders. It was her job to take them in, especially those fleeing from Raudra and Bhayanaka. If she wouldn't, with her wide-open canopy that covered everything and everyone, who would? Sringara was the most crowded land by now, everyone broken by anger and fear now hoping for some love in their lives.

Devi thanked Chaki for his help and realised today would be less a day of gazing at the sky and more one of rolling up their sleeves and helping out. She was pumped for it, that river ride had shown her just how much she was loved, and she wanted to pass it on. "Can we go find Sringara?" she said to Adbhuta and Hasya. The sisters nodded.

They made their way through the crowded streets where Devi kept bumping into parakeets and budgerigars on bicycles. Devi couldn't understand why they couldn't just fly. Frog policemen blew their whistles, directing traffic on the emerald roads.

Adbhuta handed Devi a frozen spinach cone from an ice cream cart manned by a praying mantis as they took a short cut through the park. Devi absolutely did not want to try this one, but the sisters absolutely insisted she should. Devi shook her head after one lick. Nope, there was no saving this. It tasted like spinach alright. She had no clue why people liked that green feeling on their tongues; she absolutely abhorred it. It was one of those things Ammamma was always making her eat because it was good for her and would make her grow. Ugh! For shortness sake! Adbhuta got her a green apple toffee to compensate and that was just wonderful, tangy and sweet at the same time. She munched on roast broccoli popcorn and green chilli chips wrapped up in a little paper cone, and cooled off her tongue with frozen tangy grape pops. In the sky, the sun was a cool kiwi green of the morning, and turned golden by the time they reached the border, at the foothills of the Peridot mountains.

There, nestled at the foothills, sheltered in a cavern formed by Peridot folds on three sides, at the geographical centre of the forest was a vast upside-down tree – the Cosmos Tree. It was the most beautiful tree Devi had ever seen. Its branches wove in and out of themselves like a basket that contained a whole universe. Within them sparkled the fruit of all the precious jewels in the world, emeralds, diamonds and rubies, but also black opal and tanzanite glinting in the green. Adbhuta nudged Devi and pointed out the gaps within the branches in which entire galaxies swirled in a haze of gases. Large planets orbited the trunk, which was so much wider than it looked that even though Devi kept walking round it, she still couldn't even see what was on the other side, let alone reach it. It seemed to extend endlessly, though standing in front of it, you would have thought it was just an awfully ordinary-looking wide tree in a forest.

"Except for the upside-down bit," Hasya reminded her.

Oh yes, there was that. The roots stuck up into the sky and the tendrils disappeared into the clouds. The head of the tree branched out on the ground and even beneath. It disappeared at one end under the mountain range. Or was it into it? Devi was not sure if the Peridot mountains got its colour from the tree or the tree from the Peridot.

"From the tree, we all get our colour from the tree," Hasya whispered. Devi forgot she could read her mind. It was sooo startling when she did that.

"Sorry," Hasya said, and then quickly covered her mouth.

Every now and then the tree would rumble, a tender shiver and something new, a creature, an animal, a plant, a planet would emerge from a yawning black hole and scurry away into the forest. Things were always being born out of love. It was the urge of the universe to fulfil itself that gave us new life in all forms, whether an insect or the bud of a new kind of flower. And the Cosmos tree was where all such urges flowered forth. The branches were buzzing with activity, too numerous to focus on. Stars sparkled, comets wooshed, planets formed from turbulent stardust and as they turned, celestial music arose, notes bursting into being with the sway of the motion. It was chaos of the sweetest kind. Within each of the planets was simultaneously arising vegetation, animals, people, insects and objects, oceans and mountains rose from it, entire species were created, celestial beings, *yugas* passing in the flash of an eye. Devi was mesmerised. She looked and looked for the Earth in the tree, and was pulled into its swirl until the sisters noticed and came in to pull her out. It was easy to get lost in the maze of its ornamentation if you weren't contained by mirth and wonder. Hasya pointed to a small blue dot on the top of the tree, no bigger than a blueberry.

"That's us," she said.

"That's Earth?" Devi asked, disbelieving.

The butterfly sisters nodded.

"We are so small," Devi burst out. She seemed offended and annoyed by being so insignificant to the tree. She had fully expected Earth to be some goddess somewhere on a golden branch. Where would they all fit on a blueberry?

The sisters burst out laughing.

"Ah, but you have to remember the Cosmos tree is in you," Hasya explained.

Devi scratched her head. "This is all so confusing," she protested. "The Cosmos in me? But isn't it outside me? How do I see it all every day, then? What do I see when I look up in the sky and see the stars and the sun?"

"Our minds are so vast Devi, they stretch across the known universe, and yet they are contained within us."

Devi still didn't understand it all, like then why couldn't she open her eyes and see other continents, or travel to places she wanted to visit. Yet, the more she entered the Rasa Bhugola, the more she understood there was a lot she didn't understand. And that the mystery was part of the journey. So she just shrugged and let it go.

The Cosmos tree seemed to be able to hear her thoughts too, because it trembled in agreement and dropped a big golden apple on her head. It was pretty much the tastiest and juiciest apple Devi had ever eaten.

Beneath it, Sringara, a shimmering Green Hairstreak butterfly, her wings like a silken gauze curtain, was fluttering anxiously in front of a tent of sea horses who were parched and urgently needed water. "Water, water, get them water," she was saying, as grasshoppers hopped back and forth from the river with little buckets. Frogs had formed a chain to transport buckets.

Sringara stopped to embrace Devi.

"What's happening here? Where are all these beings coming from?" Devi asked.

"Come, let me show you," Sringara said, as she rose and flew in the direction of the Peridot.

Hasya and Adbhuta picked Devi up, each holding her by one arm and followed Sringara. Up and up they went, rising above the forest floor, until they broke through the tree canopy into the unfiltered light and headed towards the far end of the Peridot mountain range. Beyond it, on the other side, Hasya said, was the land of Shanta, peace, a pristine and permanent white, where all the Rasas and colours came to rest. But Devi couldn't see above the range as they flew. However, beneath them were the mountain passes, made slushy with snow that had melted under the weary passage of travellers. Devi saw the streams of refugees – grasshoppers, ants, white reindeer, elephant, stallions, rabbits, and doves, making their way across. It was an exodus. Their wings and fur were coated with soot, they were tired and dragged their feet, clearly having walked for days, making their escape with a few meagre belongings on their backs, travelling on foot from the far ends of their burning land. Devi was horrified by what she saw. They kept flying towards the far end of the range where it merged into the Diamond range, the mountains of Shanta's land containing some of the highest peaks in the Rasa Bhugola. Sringara pointed towards the edge, where the two ranges met. The diamond edges were cracking through the Peridot's, as veins of black burst from the white heart of the mountains and rippled through like ebony rivers. Where they were touching the land of Sringara, the Earth had begun to crackle and parch, clear signs of drought.

"Look," pointed Adbhuta, as they came to a hover above the decaying landscape.

"Oh no," Devi gasped, looking at what the sisters were pointing at.

"The trees are dying."

Dried out shells of large ancient deodars and broad birches edged the hillsides and not only had their leaves fallen off, but forest fires were starting. Trees that had lasted millennia, crackling and bursting into loud flame or burning quietly with embers deep in them. As the water was being singed out of Sringara's land, it was being plunged into dryness, and the dryness brought the darkness.

"And the Cosmos Tree?" Devi gasped.

Hasya and Adbhuta looked at each other. They hadn't realised the threat was this urgent either. They had to prevent it from being parched at all costs. Any damage to the Cosmos tree would damage life in the entire world, leaving people across planets thirsty. All urge for growth in the world would cease. People would become accustomed to the darkness and sit indoors, not knowing why they were feeling this way. They needed love, more than they even knew.

There was a lot of hard work to be done. One was to find a way to house the refugees and the second was to divert the river such that it formed a moat around the Cosmos tree which could not be breached. This was of the most urgent priority. Devi saw why Sringara was in such an anxious flutter now. Sringara couldn't command the water, she was no goddess. She could only express through it when it was there. People always thought that was through making it rain or some such miracle or the other, but in fact water manifested as growth, and Sringara was in charge of seeing people grow, even when they sometimes didn't necessarily want to. And with the fire dancing closer, her expression would be stunted. If Sringara stopped, people would stop growing in many ways, not just physically, but also emotionally. They wouldn't understand things, or acquire maturity, and pass on their wisdom. They wouldn't let things go, and would hold on to grudges, becoming dry and mean and gnarly. They would be parched, like crackled Earth, and unyielding, sucking up resources. This is how the world would end. The signs were ominous.

When they got back, Devi looked around for something to carry water in and finding nothing, gathered together a few fallen banana leaves, and stitched them together with twigs, the way Ammamma used to when they had a large festival lunch. "No dishes to wash," Ammamma had winked at her, as they went gathering the leaves and twigs in the morning. She thanked her under her breath for this knowledge right now. The leaves had a natural waterproof coating which made it easy to fill. As she stitched more of them, frogs and grasshoppers came by to collect them and pass them out. They served as bowls for the water and glasses for drinking. One group of doodlebugs even went for a relaxing swim in them.

Sringara shot her a beam of gratitude. "That's really nice of you."

"No worries," Devi positively blushed. "You bring it out in me." She then sat up and tried to tug at the bank to see how she could dig a canal to make way for the water to be diverted. Moss was surprisingly hard to cut into or tear considering how soft it appeared. It was stubborn.

"Not like that silly. You have to request it first, else it won't yield," Sringara said, gently.

"Request it?" Devi muttered, puzzled. She then folded her hands, "Dear moss, can you... um... part?" she said, addressing it directly.

Hasya and Adbhuta covered up their giggles.

"Stop it you two," Sringara chided, raising her eyebrows and glaring at them. She turned back to Devi, who was looking quite lost.

"Yes, request it. It's giving up its home so you can make space for others. Moss is unyielding unless you give it what everybody wants – some gratitude. How would you feel if things are taken from you, your home, without asking?"

Devi looked stunned. Without realising it, Sringara had just named what she, what Pa were feeling, what Ammamma must have felt too before she died, the loss of a home that they had not been prepared for, taken so cruelly from them by death and changing circumstances. Nobody had asked Devi if she wouldn't mind never being able to visit the family home in Goa again. Nobody had even told her it was being sold. The next summer, when she had casually mentioned how excited she was for the holidays, to go home, that's when she knew, when it was all done. Grown-ups were constantly taking things away from children and expecting them to just be fine with it. She had literally never been asked that question before. She in fact, had never been asked for her feelings about anything. In her world, it was always she who was doing the asking. Asking for permission, asking for attention... But asking for gratitude was so off the list that she didn't even know right now what she was supposed to be feeling right now.

"Come on girls, let's show her how it's done," Adbhuta said.

Sringara, Hasya, and Adbhuta stood with their wings folded in front of them, like folded palms and addressed the goddess of the forest and its beasts, Aranyanidevi, propitiating her with an ancient hymn from the Rig Veda.

na vaa aranyaanirhantyanya-shch-ennaabh igachchhati
svaadoh phalasya jagdhvaaya yathaa-kaamam ni padyate

Aranyani does not harm, unless an enemy approaches her,
Hence, eating tasty fruit, the forest dweller settles down at will.

Aanjana-gandhim surabhim bhavana makru shiivalam
Praaham mruganaam maaataraa mara nyaaanima sham-sisham
I praise Aranyani, mother of the beasts, perfumed and fragrant,
Who offers varieties of food, though she does not till the land.

A melodious chant emerged from the sisters and Devi noticed that the forest animals and beings had joined in too, each in their own languages, until the forest was filled with a deep reverberation. Devi didn't know the words, but she folded her palms together and simply listened. She felt the deep "Auuuuuuum" rise unbidden from her middle and followed its breath rising from her navel outwards until the chants were done. The congregation of beasts and beings in the forest seemed to be connected by an expanding wave of love.

When they had finished, the forest fell still and something momentous stirred. The forest began to bristle with energy. It seemed to come alive. It seemed to understand the needs of the beings. Trees shook out the long twisty arms, and fresh glistening fruit, berries, and nuts fell off their own accord so the tired and hungry refugees could pick them off the forest floor. There was enough food for many days. Long leaves, the kind suitable for thatching roofs together gently floated to the ground. The trees wriggled off their deadwood, and pieces of timber that the tree no longer needed, bark that it had outgrown, spare branches, all that it could bear to part with, fell to the ground to enable the newcomers to build homes. The rubber tree oozed a thick sap so the beings could waterproof the homes against the rain and design the objects they needed. The Earth trembled and large boulders and clumps of clay rose out of it to be used as foundation stone or brick for the floors. And when the forest had sent these treasures, the river rose up of its own volition and turned in their direction, circumambulating the Cosmos tree, to create a protective moat out of its waters.

Sringara was shedding tears of gratitude. The three sisters bowed low to the forest floor and all the beings followed suit. Devi, watching them, copied their actions, and also felt so much awe and wonder at the love of the forest for the suffering beings of this land. She felt so touched that none had to suffer their fate alone. Perhaps, she thought, this was love, the sense that they were all in this together.

Aranyanidevi shimmered into being like a streak of green glitter spinning around the forest. The lush green of her body assembled from the confetti of fallen leaves, the breath of the forest sprung up within her as a deep resounding 'Auuuuuummm'.

Sringara, Hasya, and Adbhuta thanked her profusely. Aranayanidevi hugged them each, and when she came to Devi, she lifted her chin and kissed her on the forehead. It sent waves of rejuvenation into her until Devi felt like she had drunk some magic green juice, that made her so clean, vibrant and refreshed. As Aranyanidevi disappeared back into the dense foliage, the forest slowly returned to its rhythm and its hum. Devi blinked and looked around. All was restored to how it was, as though nothing had ever been disturbed. The magic of the forest was self-healing. No matter what was done to it, it would restore itself.

As long as the Cosmos tree was protected by the flow of the river, all would be well. As the crowd dispersed, busy in their tasks and chores for the day – there were houses to be built and food to be stored, and children to be fed – the sisters retreated to the river bank. On the promenade, a couple of caterpillars were jogging with their hundred legs, and a parakeet ran a Ferris wheel on which children were queuing up for rides. The turtle taxis were offering paddle tours of the river. The sisters and Devi grabbed a couple of honeydew melon popsicles and went for a stroll.

"I thought you guys were the goddesses of these lands," Devi said, curiously.

"We are just the presiding Rasas of these lands, Devi. We don't create or preserve them; we are simply their most potent expression. Think of us as the voice of all the beings in our lands," Sringara explained. "It would be terribly dull and monochromatic if we were all just one colour, don't you think? We are how they all speak, but we don't get to decide who speaks the loudest, or who among us is most potent."

"Then who does?" Devi asked.

"Well, it depends," Adbhuta said.

"On..?"

Adbhuta gave her one of those looks, like she should have known this. But Devi didn't.

"On what you send in to us, we just look after what you classify."

"Like sorting Lego by colour?" Devi asked.

"Yes, exactly," Hasya said.

"And the more you have of one colour of building blocks..."

"...the more of that you get to build with," Adbhuta chimed in.

"...but you only get more of one building block if you... I mean... buy maybe... collect... more of those colours," Devi saw now. It was all clicking.

"Yup yup yup," Hasya quipped.

Exactly. If you bought all green blocks, you'd have a lot of love, but you needed yellow to have wonder and what was the point of it all if you couldn't laugh? Everyone needed to laugh, to have other forms of expressions. You simply had to put it all together or you were just building a really one-sided thing. Imagine a man who only laughed all the time like a cake made out of only eggs, why, that would just be an omelette. You could never be just one thing, you had to have a little of everything.

Devi was elated by her insight. "So each time you get more and more of many things, a variety, you have more beings in your world."

"Yes. You met Laddu, the Labrador, we just gave him a voice in Adbhuta's land..." Hasya said

"Whereas, if I had been terrified by it, and it was a nasty growly angry dog, it would have gone to Bhayanaka's land."

"Exactly," all three sisters chirped together. *Now* she got it.

"So, I'm the one who's actually populating all the lands by what I do, what I interact with," Devi pondered.

"And *how* you interact with them," Hasya finished, triumphantly.

A gentle breeze began to blow across the waterfront. It was chirpy and airy and light. Devi felt such a sense of pride as she saw all the wonderful creatures and forests she had populated this world with.

Sringara caught her eye. "Right now, you're looking like that S. Ilayaraja painting 'Tamil girl with parrots'," she said. "Do you know it?"

Devi shook her head. She was sure Ammamma had told her about it. Though outwardly she seemed like a boring old normal grandmother like anyone else, Ammamma had been an artist and she knew a lot of things. She cooked and cleaned and looked after her and all of that, yes, but Ammamma had been an interesting person in her own time, and Devi suspected. The more she saw other people's grandmas, the more she realised hers was so different from them and she was so very lucky to have her. Her Ammamma was special. She read, she painted, she could tell jokes, and hold conversations, and their home was always open to people because Anil Appappan was always bringing all sorts of people home. Ammamma had met everyone from other artists and musicians to bankers and important people in the government and all kinds of holiday makers. She was the kind of person who forged connections. Devi wondered what Ammamma's Rasa Bhugola must have been like. It must have been humungous and wide and filled with sights and colours and beings of all kinds.

People always thought that being rich meant having a lot of the right things, but Anil Appappan and Ammamma weren't too wealthy. They weren't farm owners or industrialists or people who had their faces in the papers, but anyone could see they lead a life full of abundance; they were constantly giving themselves away in time, energy, attention, and kindness, and it was only the truly wealthy who were in a position to give, Ammamma always said.

The thing that always surprised Devi about Ammamma was how many people she had time for. Ammamma never missed an opportunity to listen to you, to anyone. She always stopped what she was occupied with and turned to you as though you were the most important person in the world. She had had this whole rich life before she became an Ammamma, which was why people from all over still came to her for advice. She was like an explorer but one who never left the house. Devi wanted to be like her when she grew up.

"You already are," Hasya whispered in her ear.

Devi jumped, again startled out of her thoughts.

"Look," Sringara said, "look at the end of the promenade." There in the corner was a small yellow house with a young girl in a brilliant green *pavadai*. She was playing with her pet parrots on her front porch. As Devi approached her, she turned, and Devi almost leaped back in surprise. It was her own face looking back at her, just somehow younger, more distant. The girl with the parrots couldn't seem to tell but she looked directly into Devi's eyes and smiled. It was the smile of a young girl who was fierce and confident of her own space, unafraid. There was something about her that was just so, so... Devi struggled for a word. This was one time that she could have used Hasya's help she thought. What was it? But Hasya remained silent. That was it, "powerful." Devi didn't really feel like that anymore.

Devi turned to look at Sringara. "Is that me?" she whispered.

Sringara shrugged. "It can be, it was at one time and it will be again," said Sringara. "That part of you is always here, preserved in this land."

Devi turned back to the girl. "Is she... is she... stuck here?"

"In a way," Sringara said. "You left her here until you are able to come back for her."

Devi smiled at the little girl and kissed her on the cheek. "I'm going to come back for you one day," she promised. "You will be safe here, and though you don't understand everything in the immediate moment, its meaning would come to you in its own time." She didn't explain further.

Would Sringara be safe for the little girl, Devi wondered.

"What about the black veins in the Diamond mountains? Is that the disease Chaki was talking about? Is it spreading?" she asked.

Sringara nodded sadly. "The darkness is coming for my land next because they know, if the darkness takes me over, it can suffocate the urge to grow, and once they have that, they can have it all."

Sringara's eyes flashed with determination.

"We flourish because of love, Devi. We have to keep it alive," Sringara explained.

Devi was almost too afraid to ask, but she had to know: "What happens if we fail? What happens if the darkness wins?"

Sringara looked at her wings, a beautiful gauzy green, shimmering with the unborn lights of a thousand saplings. "I will lose my wings. I will die, as will everything around me. This land and all the beings in it. All urge to multiply, to flourish, all growth, all species old and new, will be consumed." Imagining the worst and uttering those words was too much for her. Sringara broke down crying.

Adbhuta and Hasya hastened to comfort her. "That won't happen. We won't let that happen. Devi won't let that happen. We'll fight them. We promise you," they reassured her.

Devi was afraid now, but also, a little angry. Who was this who was threatening all the beauty and growth in the Bhugola? These were such happy lands, minding their own business, focussing on growth and love and light. Who had the right to do this?

Devi turned to the sisters, questions in her eyes. They looked at each other, hesitating. It would hurt her to know, but this was what she was here for, right? She couldn't change anything until she understood it all first, even if it was a bit painful to know.

Hasya gently put a wing around her shoulder as she explained. Devi was shocked. It was one of their own.

"Raudra started this and took Bhayanaka along. They are our sisters, Devi, anger and fear. Bhayanaka doesn't have the courage to do this on her own. She was recruited by Raudra, who boosted her up. They had their own lands, but they got extra fuel and realised it was quite possible for them to expand, to breach their boundaries and become bigger than they were supposed to be. They got greedy."

Devi understood. "Ammamma told me the story of the two wolves who got into a fight; the white wolf and the black wolf. One is joy and the other anger. And I asked her, Ammamma which one won, and she said the answer was 'the one who was fed'. This is like that, right?"

The sisters nodded sadly.

"Yes, Devi, exactly that. Raudra and Bhayanaka got fed more, they are getting fed more and more every day as we speak. So, they've realised they can just keep getting bigger and nobody will be able to stop them," Sringara said.

"They even began to attack us, their own sisters. I think that's the biggest betrayal of all," Hasya said, indignantly. "They are stealing our voice, want to take over and colour all our expression."

"But why were they even given their own lands?" Devi asked. "Why did we need them at all?"

"All the Rasas serve their purpose, Devi," Sringara said. "When you watch a movie don't you get angry at the villain? And how will a hero conquer a villain unless he is angry with him for what he's done?"

"Yes, or we need fear to tell us not to enter the creepy haunted house, right? I know. I keep screaming at the screen to tell them not to go into it but they just don't listen to me," Devi added, shaking her head.

"Exactly, we need fear and anger to some degree. Raudra and Bhayanaka are supposed to protect us," Hasya said. "Instead, they're the ones taking over and harming us now."

Devi remembered how Ammamma would check the tumbler of milk before handing it to her so she wouldn't scald herself while drinking it. She would pick up Devi's hand and touch it to the tumbler quickly. "Hot," she would say, pronouncing every letter, making that round scared face that meant "bad," and wag her finger so Devi learned not to touch it when it was like that. Then Ammamma would blow on it exaggeratedly. "Foo Foo," she would say and pour it from tumbler to *davara* until it became frothy and cool. She would then hold Devi's hand against the tumbler to show her it was the right temperature before giving it to her to drink. Devi was only just beginning to see how much Ammamma had protected her every day, not just from the scoldings of her parents, and from too many classes, but in so many small ways, even before she fully learned what dangers the world held for her. She understood Sringara's sense of betrayal. Imagine if Ammamma had harmed her instead. How let down she would have felt. But Ammamma wouldn't, she never could! That was the influence of love, it wanted to see another grow. And Raudra and Bhayanaka were rejecting love, rejecting Sringara. It hurt doubly.

The damage that the angry duo had done was dawning on Devi.

"Yes, it's sad. Instead of protecting us, Raudra and Bhayanaka got jealous. They thought everybody thinks of them as the villains. They didn't see what we saw, that they were vital and important too," Adbhuta said. "So Raudra got angry at everyone and began to confide in Bhayanaka. The more she expressed her anger to Bhayanaka, the more fearful they both became."

"So Bhayanaka and Raudra turned themselves into the wolves that fed off each other," Devi summed up, seeing now, how easily that could happen.

She thought she'd feel angrier at Raudra, but now she just felt sorry for her. The more she felt sorry for Raudra and Bhayanaka, the kinder she felt towards them, and their delusion. Perhaps, what they needed was not more anger but more love. As she was lost in her thoughts, a speckled grey Papillon butterfly swooped out of the forest, flew over the river, and joined them. Her wings dappled grey with orange flecks, like one of Ammamma's Diwali saris, shimmering like a Kanchivaram silk by lamplight.

"Karunya!" Hasya exclaimed, as the sisters hugged each other.

"Somebody summoned me?" Karunya asked.

Devi looked a little confused until Hasya nudged her forwards. "She did. Karunya, this is Devi. Devi, Karunya," Hasya introduced.

"Me? What did I do?" Devi asked.

Karunya explained, quite simply, "you saw." When you are able to see where people come from, why they do what they do, the things they mistakenly believe, because everyone thinks about the things they experience in their own ways, and instead of being angry at them when you wish them light, knowledge and clarity, you give birth to compassion within yourself. Compassion is the basis for mercy.

"And you cannot go into battle without mercy in your heart to begin with," Karunya finished.

"Battle? Who's going into battle? Not me! I don't have the courage for those kinds of things," Devi said.

Someone tapped her on the shoulder.

"Someone summoned me?" came a voice from behind.

Even before she turned around, Devi knew, it was Vira. Even so, she was not prepared for how stunning the sight before her was: Vira was a Palos Verdes Blue, the rarest blue butterfly in the world. Courage was a quality that not everyone summoned and while most people mistakenly looked for her in the land of Raudra, assuming that courage paired with anger, few knew that in fact, Vira and Karunya went together. They all did – Vira, Karunya, Sringara and Vibhatsa were quadruplets, born of water.

Vira was the colour of the sky in all its moods, a light rim of cloud around her edges, the darkness of the monsoon defending the plains of her wing tips, a melancholy deepening as she ran the gamut towards a sleepy mid-afternoon, bursting suddenly into the clarity of the azure. Filaments of the night ran down her arms, towards the centre, her heart, a blaze of Prussian. The more you gazed at her, the more you were pulled into her glory.

"Oh great," Vira said, rubbing her hands together in glee. "The army is assembled. Let's fight this thing."

Chapter 4

Vira Rising

The next morning, Peeli Dhoop had turned Neeli, like Ammamma turned all her uniform shirts with that magic washing liquid of hers. Devi could guess where they were going. She and Hasya tumbled through empty space and gushing air, a stretch of paddy fields soaked with water, a water slide through a large plastic elephant's open mouth, and at one point, Devi swore, a hallway with the most solemn portraits of eminent (eminently boring Devi thought) personalities on the wall, then more countryside, past a fun fair with loud music playing, a cinema hall, and then suddenly, whoosh! Hasya and Devi were coughed out of the funnel end of a long tube into what looked like a serene purply-blue ocean. Devi gasped in recognition. They had landed or splashed into 'La Mer', a large painting by an artist called Sayed Haider Raza. The painting hung in the big bank that Mom worked at.

She had seen it when Mom took her along once, and with nothing else to do, and needing to be really quiet, she had sat in front of the painting for what seemed like interminable hours, gazing at it, wondering which way was up and which was down, and in the end, even talking to it! It was quite a frustrating and lonely day. She had no clue what about it was in the least bit courageous.

As they plopped into the water, two humpback dolphins appeared from beneath the surface to lift them into the air, tossing them with their noses. Devi found herself turning a somersault and landing neatly on the back of one, as though she were a monkey in a circus. Hasya simply flew up startled and flapped her wings.

"Waaaaaaaaaaaaa," squealed Devi.

They began to skim along the surface of the ocean in leaps and bounds. Unlike the turtle taxi, the dolphins didn't offer them any seat belts and weren't very steady at the wheel. Dolphins, Devi quickly realised, seemed to quite enjoy the churn of the ocean, all its ups and downs, and set off on a race against the peaks of the waves. They leaped with exuberance, so Devi found herself high up in the air one minute and down low, almost submerged into the undercurrents, the next. Good thing she had a stomach for it or she would have felt very woozy indeed.

"Itttttt looooookkkkssss liiiiikkkkkeee yoooouuu nnnneeeeeeeddd cccccouuuuurrrrragggeee to mmmmeeeeeet Vvvvvvvvirrrrraaaaaaaah allllrigggggghhhht!" Devi went.

"Whatttttttt?" Hasya asked. But Devi didn't have the breath to repeat it. Devi realised she needed a strategy for this ride if she was to avoid feeling dizzy and sick, and so she did the only thing that made sense to her right then – she leaned back and acted like she did this every day.

"If you believe you can, you can," she said to herself, remembering Ammamma's words. At the time, she remembered arguing with her, annoyed by the advice. "It's not so easy as you think, Ammamma," Devi had whined to her, irritated. She had been struggling in particular with some homework that wasn't going anywhere. I mean, all that sounded nice but when you're faced with polynomials and fractions, then 'if you think you can, you can' doesn't really work, does it? Because, well, you can't. In these past few weeks though, Devi had kind of begun to understand what Ammamma had been trying to tell her. If you already told yourself you couldn't go there, you couldn't think this way, you couldn't see these things, solve things, have these conversations, achieve these things, you pretty much couldn't. By not admitting to the possibility of it, you sort of closed the door to things, shut yourself off from a whole world of experiences. You had to believe that all kinds of things were possible. You had to see yourself doing things you could only imagine yourself doing for you to actually be able to do them.

She thought about Mom, sitting beneath this painting every single day and not once imagining she could swim in it. So this time, Devi stopped focussing on how she had never ridden a dolphin bareback before, without stirrups or a seat belt, and decided to trust the dolphin, which would probably come back for her anyway if it dropped her, and began to look around. When you focussed on the things you couldn't do and got into a panic about not doing them, you totally missed the landscape, Devi realised. Sometimes, it took courage to just enjoy where you were.

The arms of the sky shimmered with a silvery streak lining a light blue tint that got closer, until the outlines of the brilliant azure Palos Verdes wings, its clouds flecked in cumulus patterns, emerged. Vira began to swoop and flow, flying alongside the dolphins.

"Viraaaaaaaa!" Hasya cried, waving to her sister.

Hasya and Vira met in a merry twisting embrace in the sky. If Hasya's wings set off wind chimes, Vira's set off the rumble of thunder clouds. As the sisters twirled, the sky was filled with bells and drums, a rising chant of a melody that made the landscape reverberate with ancient percussion.

As the dolphins set them down on the shore, Devi looked around. The grass as she expected, was a bluish green. The streets were paved with the kind of translucent blue boiled sugar sweets they gave you in large packets to distribute to teachers on your birthday. The kinds that never ever melted in your mouth and you finally got bored and had to chew through them, making crunching sounds that made everyone look at you and got shards lodged in your teeth that you then spent the whole day picking at with your tongue. That. It looked like glass but was hard as a rock. Devi knelt down and peeped through the road beneath her feet. There was nothing but endless swirls of sticky blue bubbling upwards like candy lava.

Adbhuta whirled out of the sky and Karunya and Sringara followed. The sisters were racing ahead now and Devi had to run to catch up.

Clickety clack clickety clack her shoes went against the blue. Vira's land was by the sea. As she ran, to her left were the endless rolling blue hills, their sides bedecked with forests of teal eucalyptus trees, whose oil scented the air. And to Devi's right stretched the shore along the lapis lazuli ocean. She stood mesmerised by the alternating colours.

Hasya and Adbhuta shouted, "Come on, you'll miss the show!"

"The show? What show?" Devi called, tearing herself from the scene and following them down to a strip of beach on which a whole host of blue beings had gathered.

"Today is the benediction of the blue moon."

On the beach was a gathering like she had never seen before. There were blue horses, sapphire unicorns and bejewelled peacocks. Overhead hovered blue jays, hyacinth macaws, and purple honeycreepers with their curved bills. Devi looked down and at her feet was a family of blue bullfrogs.

"Croaaaak. Excuse me," the bullfrog man said, "some space please. You almost stepped on my little boy."

"Oh, I'm so sorry I didn't see you there," apologised Devi.

"That's okay miss, we all want a good view," bullfrog man said.

"Stay with us, when moon starts rising, we'll lift you up between us," Adbhuta said.

"Does the moon rise in the middle of the day often?" Devi asked.

"No, just once in a blue moon."

"Of course, why did I not know that?"

"And why are we standing here?"

"Why, we are blue moon bathing, of course."

"Of course. Um, why?"

"Well, you see blue is not a colour that actually occurs in Nature. It's actually a trick of the light. Blue is a reflection, it's a way of seeing. You only notice it at a particular angle. We see the blue when we comprehend blue. More often than not, the pigment gets washed out by the strength of the sun," Adbhuta said.

"Did you know Devi, that this land is also Vibhatsa's land? The land of aversion," Sringara said.

"Vibhatsa's? What about Vira's?"

"They're twins, and they are so close they share each other's land," Sringara said.

Devi considered that. They seemed such an unlikely pair, almost the opposite of each other. It seemed to Devi that Vibhatsa turned away from everything, while Vira ran towards things. How could they be twins who were that close? Devi didn't understand how that would work.

"Those of us who are different, we get called the freaks, the fringe, the odd ones. We are the ones who most lack courage to be ourselves. We turn blue, despondent," Vira said. She gestured with her wings down the beach. "People call us 'unnatural'. They make us feel like we don't belong."

Devi still looked like she didn't get it. Vira gently turned to her.

"So, guess who needs the most courage to walk in the world as they are?"

Devi understood what Vira was saying.

She knew people in her class, those who are left-handed, those who coloured outside the lines, those who were shy, who stammered, who were friends with everyone they were not 'supposed to' be friends with (because, you know, as Ammamma used to say, there's just no one you're not supposed to love though some people thought there were), the ones who are never welcome anywhere.

Julie Ammamma and Anil Appappan had met in college. Appappan had dropped out to run his father's farm while Ammamma had gone on to art school. So technically she was more educated than Appappan, but in so many ways, they were equals, Ammamma would say. Most importantly, Julie was a Christian, and Appappan was a Hindu. And there were people who hadn't liked that they had gotten married. So Appappan's father had disowned him, said he wouldn't get the farm if he married her. Appappan had walked away and married her anyway. They had lived off her paintings for a while, until they saved enough to buy a small plot of land in Goa. And then as the farm grew, Appappan expanded it until it became the big house they had all loved as home. Ammamma loved to tell Devi this story. But the bit she loved to tell the most was of how brave Appappan had been. "You had to be too," Devi would say to her. Ammamma would smile. "Ah, but I was gaining my whole world," she would say. There was a time when it was difficult. Ammamma used to describe it as their 'blue years'. They didn't know where the money would come from. Ammamma was still in college, where would they live. But they managed, even though the whole world was against them, they managed. "How Ammamma, how did you manage?" Devi would ask. Ammamma would smile. "Because in all the blue we had a small glimmer of warmth between us, like a spark of a fire, a heart of saffron, that we couldn't allow to be put out, so we protected it," she said. So Devi knew what Vira meant when she said the courage came through the despair.

Devi recalled the stories of Lord Shiva Ammamma used to tell her, about how he gathered all those who lived in the fringes of society, the outcasts, those sent to the cemeteries, the ones who never got invited to anything, got left out, and loved them all as his own. And because people weren't very nice to him because he kept such 'odd' company, he went off and lived among his 'odd' entourage himself. He was kind of a pretty cool god that way. That's why Shiva was blue. He embraced all the oddness of the world, all its despair, and took it on himself. That's why Ammamma loved to paint him.

"Those who live with all that judgement, they're the ones in whom courage naturally occurs. It's like finding a diamond inside a lump of coal," Vira said.

"Saffron ore within the blue mountain, the flickering fire in the cold," Devi whispered, awed by the thought.

"Precisely. Without those who live their own glorious lives just the way they are, there is no courage in the world. I am born inside them."

"Perhaps," Devi said, "we need to stop classifying them as Vibhatsa, aversion, then? If we called them all brave, there wouldn't be any revulsion at all. Why should anyone have to face it at all?"

That was a great question. The point was, Vira explained, beings weren't born courageous. What was the point when there was nothing to be courageous about? There was only any sense in feeling brave about conquering your blues, when there were blues to conquer. So, we had to first see the aversion, the disgust, because seeing that taught us so much about the world we lived in and ourselves.

"When we see the aversion outside ourselves, in society, we see what people genuinely think and feel about them. That tells you a lot about people," Vira said. It showed you who was being honest and inclusive and genuinely compassionate, and who was just faking it.

Devi thought about all the times people had liked her *kolam* pictures, or her drawings. She was always trying harder and harder, and looking to see if people liked what she was doing. But she also knew she loved her drawings so she kept at it anyway. It hadn't occurred to her that somebody might dislike it because, well, they were in a bad mood or something. That it might be something in them that made them find a flaw in her. If people disliked something she did, she had always thought that meant she wasn't good enough. She thought of Ammamma who wasn't a very famous artist but how she quietly did her work every day, standing at her easel, and painting away. Imagine if Ammamma had thought, "Well, all these really famous people don't think I'm very good so maybe I should stop trying." She didn't. She painted because it made her happy, and if you thought about it, that was a very courageous thing to do.

Devi thought about how hard it must be to be Sapna, the girl who came to school in a wheelchair, or Padmini, who walked with a cane because she was blind, or Sheila, who was so much taller than everyone else in class that people called her a giant, or Rahul, whom everyone whispered was 'gay' because he just seemed so different from all the other boys. People like that, who chose to express themselves differently, who had a different voice, were always being picked on and laughed at. People treated them with aversion. They didn't sit next to them in class or on the bus, or share their lunches with them, or invite them to their parties. Devi understood aversion well, she'd seen so many people live with it. And she kind of understood that seeing that aversion made all these people not like the ones who made fun of them. Vibhatsa helped you sort those kind of people out.

"Perhaps," Devi said, after giving it a good think, "we treat ourselves with aversion before anyone else can."

Vira agreed, shaking her head sadly. "That's so true Devi. We do take what people say about us to heart and think we're no good. Vibhatsa does that sometimes. I tend to go the other way and push past it. It can take a while to overcome that."

"How?" asked Devi, "It must be so hard to overcome that on your own when sometimes your own parents or friends are telling you everything you are or that you do is wrong and bad and disgusting."

Sringara hugged Devi. "That's why we are all here. We live inside everyone. Even if others don't direct love and wonder and mirth towards you, you know you have us."

"It would take a lot of courage to... Ooooooh I SEEEEE NOW where courage comes from," Devi said, her eyes opening wide and almost jumping up and down with joy. "I GET IT NOW."

Courage in the midst of aversion, thought Devi, was like the fragile stamen in the heart of the saffron flower that she'd watched a documentary about. It was so painstakingly grown and harvested by hand, and in the end, it became the rarest and most sought-after spice in the world. You had to go through all those fields of blue to get to its saffron heart.

"You find the courage by pushing past all the aversion that people throw at you and that you throw at yourself. And, by filling all your other lands with colour. When you fill yourself with wonder, mirth, and love, going through the blue gets easier. That's also how you grow, that's why Vibhatsa is a water butterfly," Sringara explained.

"I get it," Devi said. "It's just seeing things in a different light."

Ammamma used to say you don't get a pearl until a bit of sand gets inside the oyster and irritates things around a bit. But the oyster with the pearl is the one that gets called the odd one. It's only years later they realised they were the precious one. And that realisation was the hard part.

"Exactly," Hasya said. "These blue beings, they are the storehouse of the most courage in the world. But it can be hard sometimes to be different, to stand up to the world, to not be what people expect you to be, and cope with those who treat you with disgust, fear and hate. But here's the thing that nobody tells us, Devi. You find your courage when you push past the blue and find the rare ore inside it all."

Vira bristled a little.

"What now?" Hasya asked.

"Nothing."

"What? Tell me! Well you're thinking something so you may as well tell me now because you're going to give me a piece of your blue mind later, anyway."

"Courage is not as rare as people think you know," Vira grumbled under her breath.

"Howzzat?" Devi asked.

"Well, we exist everywhere, it's just that you have stopped looking at us and recognising us. You people look at everything in naked sun burned light of day. Blue requires a special perspective. You have to reflect us. When you don't, it seems like we cease to exist. You look for us only in superheroes and stuff like that. It takes courage for a lot of people to get up and go about their daily lives when in fact they're quite afraid of the world. Kids who go to school knowing there are bullies and thugs lurking. Or those who are scared of monsters. People who've been told they're different because of their skin or birth or wealth, and not good enough. The world is so intimidating for so many people."

"...or those of us who stay home alone when our parents are not there or when we've lost a grandparent," Devi offered.

"Precisely. So really, we're everywhere, you just don't see us. But you have to see us, really see the blue," Vira said.

They were interrupted by a gasp that rose from the congregation.

Devi was transfixed by what was happening on the horizon. A gentle blue tinged light was beginning to spread from the tip of the orb that was beginning, ever so smoothly, to rise.

There it was: The Blue Moon.

A sapphire gleaming in ice crystals that looked like it was wearing a coat of diamonds.

"Wow," Devi gasped. "She is spectacular."

The whole congregation on the beach, in the streets, in the windows of their houses, was hypnotised by the rise of the scintillating orb. Something within Devi was stirring. On this special rise day, the moon seemed so close to Earth that it felt like you could reach out and touch its face. When in fact, she was reaching out and touching yours.

A stillness fell over everything. The bullfrog family urged their children to spread out their arms and legs so all of them could be bathed in the serene blue light that began to spread across the land. Devi looked to the left and right and turned to look behind her. Every living creature with an inch of blue on it had gathered on the beach. There were blue lobsters and starfish, and blue crabs. There were blue ladybirds and slugs and snails, blue grasshoppers and dragonflies and moths. In the water ahead of them, the blue whale made its presence known by its periodic puffs through its water spout and the marlin rose its sharp pointed snout in salutation to the rising moon. Like a spreading inkblot, a deep blue light raced along the rays and stained everything with its colour. As they stood there, Devi noticed, everything blue began to be strengthened. The hills turned a shade deeper and the eucalyptus leaves shivered and released a stronger essence, spreading its bouquet till all of the land smelled like Ammamma's bathwater.

As all the blue became replenished, the skies turned Prussian and the colour spilled over the edges of the clouds and began to pour like an ink rain. A huge cheer went up and all the assembled beings began to cheer and dance in the sudden downpour. Devi noticed that Hasya too, all gold and silver and rose, was giving off a hint of a blue sparkle.

"You're blue too," Devi cried, shouting to be heard amidst the cheers.

"So are you!" Hasya shouted back.

Devi looked down at herself; she was sparkling and shining in so many shades of blue. Suddenly, she noticed her white school uniform was blue too.

"Yaaaaaaaaaaaaaaaaaaaaaa!" she yelled, covering her mouth with horror.

"What happened?" Adbhuta asked.

"The uniform," Devi said gesturing frantically towards her dress. It was all inky blue! She was going to be in so much trouble!

Adbhuta and Hasya held wings and laughed at her until Devi realised it was quite funny too, and joined in.

"You look like The Little Girl in Blue," Vira teased.

"Whossat?" Devi asked.

"It was a little girl who was painted by a famous artist, Amrita Sher-Gil. She didn't want to pose but was forced to by her mum, but her mum then thought the painting didn't look like her and didn't want it. So the artist took it back and pretended to get rid of it but secretly kept it. And now it's one of the most famous paintings in the world," Adbhuta explained.

Devi considered this. Sometimes, she thought, we looked at the things that happened to us as bad, but they just turned us into the absolute special, most unique versions of ourselves, even if we couldn't understand that while it was happening to us and were sulking throughout.

Devi decided she was going to enjoy being turned into a little girl in blue after all.

Then, she saw Vira. While everything else had turned a deeper blue than it originally was, Vira had turned a deep and vibrant red and orange, the shade of saffron. Her wings of midnight blue had shimmered and transformed until she caught the moonlight and glinted golden within the heart of a sea of blue.

From Vira's fallen wings rose Vibhatsa, now the Palos Verdes who took Vira's place. Vibhatsa and Vira were more than just twins, they were each other's shadow, one emerging from the other, one couldn't rise without the other. And they now did tumble turns and cartwheels together, a beautiful Blue Moon dance in the luminous sky.

All the beings, children, elders, from sea horses to bullfrogs and elephants, played in the rain until the moon rise had lit up the whole sky. Then, they went to the ice cream man and bought themselves frozen jamun popsicles and found the popped bluecorn man.

"We just call this popcorn," Devi protested.

"That's because you just have white and yellow popcorn there," Adbhuta said. "Eat this and see."

The popcorn seemed quite normal tasting to Devi except that once she put a piece into her mouth it began to turn her a deep shade of blue. But she was the only one who couldn't see it.

"What? What?" she kept asking as the sisters burst out laughing. Then she looked down and saw her hands and feet.

"Take another," Hasya said. So she did, and she turned orange. Orange to blue, blue to orange she went, one after the other.

"Wow, I could do this all day," she said, and took another.

"You really need a new word for 'wow,'" Hasya said to her sister.

"I never get tired of it," Adbhuta said.

"Hey, I've been meaning to ask. How come you came to get me and not Adbhuta or Vira, you know, if this is her land," Devi asked Hasya.

"Why she's our messenger of course. Mirth is always the finest messenger," Vira replied. "That's why her wings are not white, she isn't only a communicator of her own joy, but that of all of us, she wears the insignia of the messenger of the joy of wonder, the joy of love, the joy of courage..."

"...of Aversion? Anger? Fear? How does that work?" Devi interrupted. "That makes no sense. There's no joy in them."

Adbhuta put her wing on Devi's shoulder. "You enjoy drawing your *kolams* don't you?"

"Of course. They're my memory of Ammamma."

"So you enjoy thinking about connecting with her, even if it makes you a bit sad, maybe even a bit angry, or fearful of staying home without her?"

Devi nodded. She began to feel the tremor of anger rise in her again. As it did, Devi noticed, the land of Vira and Vibhatsa began to tremble and shake a little. But Devi wouldn't give up that link for anything. Even though Ammamma was gone, she enjoyed the memory, even if it did envelop her in grief sometimes.

"Don't wallow," Mom would say, but sometimes, she enjoyed the wallowing.

"All of us, the nine sisters, the navarasas, Adbhuta, Sringara, Vira, Karunya, Vibhatsa and me," Hasya began to list them, "and of course, you know all about Raudra and Bhayanaka, have a little bit of each other in us."

"Wait that's only eight. Who's number 9?"

A silence fell over the group.

"That's Shanta, tranquillity," Vira offered. "She's imprisoned. She's the one we're battling to free."

"Imprisoned?" Devi said, surprised.

"Yes, in the heart of her own land. She has now been ringed in by a circle of fire formed by Raudra, and Raudra in turn has defended herself with a ring of terror," Vira said. She looked despondent. She'd been studying the lay of the battleground for some time now.

Devi looked perplexed. Ring of fire? Sisters against sisters? How? Why? It was all too much.

"It's difficult to explain. Come I'll show you," Vira said.

"But where are we going," Devi wanted to know.

"Up there," Vira said, gesturing upwards. "For a bird's eye view."

"But why can't we just fly up now," Devi wanted to know. As in, they all could, and they could just carry her.

"It's too dangerous," Vira said. Raudra was close to Vira's land, just at the borders, across the Nilgiri mountains. They couldn't risk it.

Hasya didn't want to go at all. She insisted she was really really thirsty and wanted to go for a drink and threw such a tantrum, they had to go her way. They found a stall handing out cold blue pea iced tea with ice cubes shaped like fish that clinked together in the glass.

When they had finished, they made their way to the air field where giant blue hot air balloons offered rides over the blue mountains, once a favourite pastime of the blue people. The balloons weren't in use anymore. Vira had forbidden venturing too close to the mountains. She didn't want her beings, who were naturally courageous, to be lured into fighting for the wrong team. Beings could be like that, rush off all courageous without knowing the lay of the land, or seeing what dangers really lurked out there. They were constantly courageously singing when they couldn't hold a note, or falling in love when they didn't know the person, or going off on adventures without a map, or saying things that got them into trouble, which was not what courage was about at all. Courage, true courage, Vira explained, only came with deep self-knowledge, both internal and external.

Vira commandeered a balloon.

"Come on, let's go," Devi said. She'd never been up in a hot air balloon before.

Hasya hesitated. "It's getting late."

"But you said there was no time over here, it's perfectly possible to..." Devi protested. "What is up with you? What's wrong? Why are you being so difficult today?"

Adbhuta said, "Come on Hasya, we have to show her sometime."

"Show me what?" Devi insisted.

Hasya turned to her sister, "I just don't think she's ready yet."

"Ready for what, Hasya? Tell me. I'm ready," Devi said.

Adbhuta said nothing. Hasya turned to look at her.

"The darkness."

Devi blinked.

She would later blame it on Vira's presence of course, inspired by Hasya's own outburst, but Devi had found the courage to throw an equally massive tantrum and the Rasa sisters had been wonderstruck by it. Her Mom would have just walked away, one of the advantages of being in the Rasa Bhugola, Devi thought.

"Impressive," Adbhuta said, genuinely struck with wonder.

Hasya still grumbled but they all loaded themselves into a brilliant blue hot air balloon that seemed to merge into the sky the higher it rose so no one could see it from the ground. From down there it just looked like a couple of dots bobbing up in the sky. Vira was steering.

"A lot of wonder only when we look closely," Adbhuta said.

Hasya was still quite unsure about all of this.

As the Nilgiris came into sight, towards the east, above the crests and peaks of the range, Devi could see lightning flashing amidst the eddying pool of fury.

"DON'T look directly into the swirl," Vira warned, and Adbhuta, who was quite tall, positioned herself between Devi and the direction of the darkness, facing her so Devi was looking into her eyes instead. Adbhuta turned her wings opaque so Devi could no longer see past or through them.

Devi reluctantly turned away. She was curious. She did want to see, wasn't that why they were up here? What was all that about anyway?

"Does this have something to do with why you came to find me?" Devi asked.

Hasya looked at Devi and nodded.

"Then why won't you tell me? How can I know what to do unless you tell me?" Devi asked.

Adbhuta sighed. "She's right you know. We could be making it worse and worse as we speak. And besides, we're there with her now. What is the worst that could happen?"

Hasya looked sharply at her sister. "You know the worst that could happen, don't you? Don't ask me to risk that again."

She turned to Devi. "You have to promise, absolutely promise you won't look where we tell you not to look. It's imperative that I can trust you to trust us."

Devi nodded. "Absolutely. I trust you."

Adbhuta removed the filter of opacity over her wings but left them outspread.

"Look through the window of Adbhuta's wings only," Vira cautioned her. "Do not look directly at the clouds, at that land, at the swirl, nothing."

"Got it," said Devi. "Like a solar eclipse. Will my eyes be hurt by its rays if I look right at it?"

Adbhuta said, "Nope. Much worse. You'll be sucked right into it."

Hasya added in a shaky voice. "And we're very afraid we won't be able to get you back."

Looking through the filter of Adbhuta's wings, Devi looked at the ugly seething mass of a storm brewing. It looked like a volcano readying to erupt in the sky. From its flashing core periodically spurted tendrils of darkness that reached out over the horizon and took a chunk off this mountain top and that tree. Lightning smashed the tops of buildings, and entire trees went up in smoke. In the flashes appeared clouds of memories, people's faces, events, places that seemed vaguely familiar to Devi though she couldn't be too sure from this distance. It rained a heaty acid rain, steaming venomous droplets, on to the land below that was getting more and more parched. It looked like a terrible, terrible place. Within its heart lay the pristine and serene white core of icy mountains, withstanding great heat and this terrible fury, majestically, all on its own, its white peaks still proud, visible from the balloon. From the hot air balloon, as and when the storm fell momentarily silent, Devi could hear the cries of the beings trapped in that land, voices pleading for someone to hear them, asking to be set free.

Devi shut her ears instinctively. The land was powerful even through the filter. Devi could see why Hasya was afraid of exposing her to it. It was easy to be sucked right into the spell of darkness. Once you looked into its heart, it was like an abyss, you just kept falling in.

"Don't worry," Vira said, her voice authoritative, taking command of Devi's attention.

"Remember you have a powerful tool with you to dispel any reverberations that you don't want around you on your own," Hasya reminded her.

"What is that?" Devi asked.

Unbidden, the Aaaauuuuuuuuummmmmmm began to rise from her insides, resounding against her inner walls, creating a protective aura of sound inside her that emanated outwards.

Instantly soothed by it, this warm buzzing in her tummy, Devi took her attention from the stormy land and followed the Aaaauuuuuuuuummmmmmm and the path of the cool breath inside her for a while. It began below her navel and made itself a path through her middle, upwards towards her chest, where it shook the loudest, travelling up towards her nose, where it released the breath and exhausted itself into the air around her. Devi followed it twice, and when she opened her eyes, she saw the storm, though still where it was in the distance, it seemed to have lost some of its power over her, and seemed less menacing. Its thundering voice was far diminished, and the air immediately around her was pulsing blue again.

Vira looked at Hasya.

"See," she said. "She's ready."

Devi looked through Adbhuta's wings to the stormy land, this time with fearless and clear vision. The churn was threatening to cross the blue boundaries. It had already seeped further towards its right, into the pale sliver of green that connected the two lands, already making inroads into Sringara, more than they had noticed the last time. Several more parts of it were facing an unheralded autumn, the steady encroaching of dying leaves.

"That's Sringara's land," Hasya said, sadly. "It's drying up at the edges. Raudra is progressing."

"...And there?" Devi said, pointing to the snow-capped mountain peaks in the far distance, over which the cloud of Raudra hovered, the blackened and charred forests along its sides sparking now and then into embers.

Hasya said nothing. She didn't trust her voice to speak.

"That's Shanta's land, tranquillity. It's completely destroyed. They're taking over the whole Bhugola," Adbhuta said, without turning around, keeping her focus on Devi's line of vision.

"If they succeed, they'll take over the whole world," Adbhuta added.

Devi gasped.

"We have to rescue Shanta," Hasya said, her heart pining for her eldest sister. "That is the only way out."

Devi didn't want to upset her, but she had to ask.

"How do you know Shanta is okay?"

Hasya smiled and pointed to the flowing river.

"All hope isn't lost yet."

The river was formed from the melting of Shanta's heart, high up in the highest peaks of the diamond mountain range. As long as the river melt was steady and clear, its waters flowing, she was still alive. It was what sustained all the other Rasa lands, kept them in balance and connected them. Shanta was no longer reachable, she was completely surrounded by the ring of Raudra who was in turn surrounded by Bhayanaka, but this was the sign they had that she was safe.

What the sisters knew but hadn't told Devi was that the melt had been steadily increasing. The water level in the river had started rising a little bit every day. Which meant that Shanta was holding out but was at risk. It was imperative they reach her soon. Before she was all thawed out and taken over by the blaze.

"The Rasa Bhugola's people mirror each other. It's very easy for what's in one to spread like a contagion. Mirth begets mirth and wonder begets wonder but also, fear and anger beget fear and anger. It echoes through," Adbhuta explained.

"The darkness that spreads in one, spreads in another," Devi said, softly.

"That's how the darkness is beginning to spread through the world," Hasya said.

"What about all the goddesses now? Why aren't they stopping Bhayanaka and Raudra?" Devi wanted to know. Surely if the Rasas were only expressions, someone was in charge here. They set the rules, maintained the boundaries, provided them with a wild and wonderful populace of beings, kept the order. Who was in charge?

The sisters looked at each other. Devi was right. They were only the voices of what the goddesses sent their way. They were the true queens of the highest realms.

"The goddesses live in the Lotus Palace high up on the Diamond Mountains, in the heart of Shanta's land. Until we release Shanta, they will remain imprisoned. They can't emerge in that kind of weather, they would be singed," Adbhuta explained, diverting Devi's attention to the highest peaks of the range, jutting up just through and above Raudra's cloud. Raudra was up to their neck and Shanta had been driven higher and deeper into her own kingdom for refuge. All routes of escape had been cut off.

"Also why we can't be reckless, in case they harm the goddesses," Vira said.

"Why doesn't anyone rescue them?"

"For now we have been battling to secure our own lands. We have an obligation to preserve what has been put into our charge, Devi, that is our primary duty," Sringara explained. Devi thought about the Cosmos tree. So much long-term damage would ensue if any aspect of each of their lands was lost in the battle for Shanta.

"There's one more thing, Devi. Our beings don't have permission to cross the borders. We can't assemble an army until the goddesses lift the boundaries. We butterflies can collaborate but the beings cannot get past the powerful spells that keep them in their places," Hasya explained.

There would be anarchy in the Rasa Bhugola if the beings of Adbhuta crossed over into the land of Raudra. The moment they stepped across the border, all the wonder would become laced with rage, and the whole perspective would tilt and wobble, throwing the mind into chaos. Balance required them to keep the beings of the Bhugola where they were.

"Then who can save the goddesses? Who is the grown up here? Who casts the spell? Who is in charge of keeping the Rasas in their place?"

The sisters looked at each other and then at Devi. The expressions on their faces, bewilderment. They each looked a little sad.

"We thought you knew," Adbhuta said.

"What? What did I know?" Devi asked.

"You do, Devi. You run the Bhugola. It is all in your mind. You're the one who is in charge," Hasya spoke up.

Devi stepped back, shocked, and sat down cross-legged on the floor of the basket of the hot air balloon. She put her head into her hands. It was all so much to take in. She? In charge? She was just a kid. Her parents should be in charge. Her Ammamma. Her teachers. She didn't know how to make decisions. And if she did, how did she not know this?

How had she allowed her world to come to this?

"It's not your fault, Devi," Hasya consoled her. "You didn't know. You were never taught to look inwards. You didn't know you were in charge of all this."

Devi had always had someone else making all the decisions for her, from what to wear and what time to wake up and play, and now, to be told that she was the one who was supposed to know where it all went, how it got ordered, and keeping the Rasas all equal was in her charge, she was a little overwhelmed.

"How can I be that?" Devi asked. All she knew about goddesses were those clay statues she prayed to during festivals, mostly to be able to get to the feast laid out for them, the *bhog*.

"The goddesses, aren't they the divine beings with magical powers who grant us wealth and education and purpose? How do I have anything to do with liberating them? They are the ones who have to liberate and uplift me. Who am I to protect goddesses and entire worlds?"

Devi fell into a panic. If these worlds were dependent on her to liberate them, then surely they were all doomed. Maybe Hasya was right, she was just not ready for all this. Young women couldn't inherit kingdoms they knew nothing of and be expected to save them.

"Don't worry, Devi," cooed Hasya, soothingly, "we are all on your side. You have us with you. You're not alone."

But in that moment, no matter what Hasya said, Devi not only felt very alone, she felt very guilty and hurt by the ways in which she had let them all down. She felt the cold blue light of Vibhatsa fill her up, and somewhere deep inside, a small flicker of red rage and black fear, at being so very alone. No matter what Hasya or Adbhuta or Sringara said, the blue had begun to creep up on her. And she couldn't see Vira at all. She had disappeared, merged with the backdrop of the sky that reflected back to Devi exactly what she was feeling: an aimless wandering that had no clear outcome.

"I think I'd like to go back now please," she said to Hasya.

Devi made it to school in time for the early bell though the class teacher did remark that her mother was putting too much liquid blue into her uniform wash these days and maybe she should tone it down a bit? Beyond that, nothing gave Devi's secret adventure away. In her mind's eye though, now and then, just when she was busy solving a sum, or out on the playground with her friends, or on the bus ride home, would flash a stormy whirl, black and red and mesmerising.

Chapter 5

Wake Up Vibhatsa

Devi had fallen into a pattern of waking up early, drawing the *kolam* with her chalks and asking everyone, from Mom and Pa to neighbour aunty and the milkman and now the watchman, the little kids from the floor above on their way to their bus stand, their ayah, the vegetable vendor and anyone else who had places to go in the morning, to take a moment to stand and gaze at her creations. She hoped she was kindling a sense of awe in them. And though her neighbours and family couldn't always summon it, they often pretended to, out of compassion and love. Devi saw that you couldn't make someone feel awe or wonder or show it. Their Bhugolas were all their own. These days, that wasn't enough for Devi.

So, Devi asked Mom to make an Instagram page for her, since she wasn't allowed to have one for herself. She could use it to update pictures of her daily *kolams*.

"It serves a double purpose, Mom," Devi explained, trying her hardest to convince Mom to let her have it. "One, if I know people are expecting daily update, I'll probably be more regular at it. And second, well, you never know, I might become famous!"

Mom laughed, and after some cajoling, she did help Devi make her page, though she was only strictly allowed to access it from Mom's phone and only under the condition that Mom would have the password so she could check in on it at any time. Devi gleefully agreed. Soon enough, the page attracted a number of followers who were all interested in the *kolams* Devi was drawing. She found a small community of enthusiasts who gave her suggestions and tagged her on posts so she also got a steady flow of design ideas to further get inspired by. Devi thought she also liked the idea of connecting the dots, it just seemed a pretty cool thing to do. Some mornings she would imagine they were constellations and using an astronomy chart that she had made Pa download and print for her, she would connect them in the shapes of the stars. This morning was the big dipper.

"What is that? I can't understand what it is. It looks very nice though. Just, what is it? Is it a shopping cart from the supermarket?" Dharmendar the milk man asked.

He was the most honest critic. Admittedly, he could be a bit severe at times, but nevertheless Devi appreciated honesty; it was better than those who just said 'nice nice' and didn't really mean it. So she sincerely looked forward to his feedback.

She meant Mom and Pa of course, who were constantly running out of wonder, even more than they ran out of coffee powder. They would sometimes absent-mindedly say "good good" or "spectacular" or "outdone yourself today" on their way out the door and Devi could tell they hadn't really looked. Not really.

It didn't matter so much. Thanks to her trips to the Bhugola, she knew not everyone saw everything with a sense of wonder and to have it all the time made it not so very special. So, she was okay with it. Besides, she thought, the purpose of this was different. It was her secret letter between herself and Ammamma.

So, if she was a bit unsure of her design, she would look at it and ask herself, "what would Ammamma do?" and try very hard to channel Ammamma's sense of wonder when she didn't have her own to fall back on. Ammamma's Bhugola was so rich, Devi felt like she could draw upon her memory of it. This was how an inheritance of tradition worked, or ought to. She found that was what invariably gave her the best response, the one with which she knew what to really do. For instance, it could get confusing if Dharmendar liked it but Ammamma wouldn't, then it would need to be redone and that was that. But if Ammamma liked it and Dharmendra and neighbour aunty or Mom and Pa didn't, then it would stay regardless. Ammamma was the decision maker. The Big Dipper would stay. She loved it. Ammamma loved it. If she were here, they would have gone down for a walk after dinner or sat on the balcony when her legs were aching and draw outlines of the stars in the sky with their fingers.

It was sometime since she had called Hasya now, about ten days. It wasn't that she didn't miss the Rasa sisters or wasn't fascinated by the goings-on in the Rasa Bhugola, but she had a lot on her plate right now. Mid-terms were coming, and there were so many assignments due. Mom had also held good to her promise of sticking her in more what she called "outgoing activities" and soon enough Devi found herself prancing about in what she could only describe as an old swim suit with cycling shorts and a tutu in front of the mirror of a giant.

"Who needs to learn ballet in Mumbai, Neela?" Pa had grumbled when he heard the class fee.

"Arre, you don't want her to have refined tastes or what?" Neela shot back. "Only our child should be a bumpkin or what?"

"What next, you're going to put her in an opera appreciation class?"

"What do you know? Did you know the other day there was an article in the paper about a boy from the lower income area who got talent hunted and received a full scholarship to Julliard."

"I assure you Neela, if Devi gets admission to Julliard and we don't have the money to pay for it, I will sell the house and the shirt off my back to send her there, but I somehow don't think ballet is the thing for her."

Devi, who had been eavesdropping from her room, while simultaneously attempting to disrobe from this conglomeration of costumes after her trial class, got her legs stuck in the entanglement of the swimsuit and cycling shorts and chose this moment to crash into her dresser, sending most of the items on it tumbling to the ground.

Mom rolled her eyes.

"You never know it will give her some grace. Maybe she will be a little less clumsy after she takes a few classes."

"I ... uhhhhhh... heard .... Aaaaargh get this thing off of me..... dat," Devi shouted from inside her room. "Who you guys calling clumsy, hunh? I have a following on Instagram okay? I'm an *influencer* now."

Pa rolled his eyes now. "Okay, whatever it takes to keep her off the internet, let her attend it."

Mom bent over the counter top and kissed Pa on the cheek before hurrying to rescue Devi from herself.

"I get no respect around here," Devi grumbled, her head stuck in the hand hole of her t-shirt and her cycling shorts entangled around her ankles. Mom laughed and ruffled her hair. Unfair move. She couldn't even push Mom's hand away, she was so stuck, good and proper. The good thing about all these classes was Devi was making new friends and had tonnes of gossip to share about who said what and who wouldn't sit next to whom and who brought what stinky thing in their tiffin box so the class had to shut down and move to the hall while they aired out the room.

"You're a laugh a minute," Mom said. "I'm so glad you're opening up. That break did you good."

Devi suddenly felt a deep sadness gush over her. She thought of Hasya, who had come to get her when she needed her the most. But when Hasya and Adbhuta and Sringara had shown her their land was in trouble, what had she done? She had avoided them. She found herself drawing upon the inheritance of Ammamma's Bhugola instead; it was vibrant enough to nourish her, even all the way over here, so long after her passing. Devi felt a surge of guilt and shame. Instantly, her feet turned to lead and the swirling storm flashed upon her inner eye. She shuddered and shut her eyes quickly, to blink out the heavy sensation it was leaving her with.

"What happened?" Mom said, alarmed.

Devi shook the image out of her head quickly. "Nothing, I think I'm just really tired now."

"It has been a long day and you're not used to all this activity. Come on, we have some special pasta for dinner today."

"Yay!" said Devi. Though she was thrilled to not be eating more of the roti sabzi dal chawal boring stuff, some of the thrill, she had to admit, was feigned. She couldn't summon up butterflies in a bucket full of feelings right now.

Mom looked at her and thought to herself, maybe she was overloading her out of her own need to keep her busy. Inexplicably, her feet felt heavy and her stomach sank. She felt a pang of guilt and shame too. Since nobody else was too chatty that night, and Pa wasn't particularly a fan of pasta, he never understood what exactly it was, it looked like children's party food to him and why were they having it for dinner? Etc. etc. he grumbled all through dinner. Nobody ate very much that night. The atmosphere at dinner was exhausting and gloomy.

"Is it okay if I don't do my *kolam* in the morning?" Devi asked. "I'd like to sleep in for once. Do you think Ammamma would mind?"

Mom, suddenly feeling the heaviness in her own shoulders, the weight of work and home and so many things to do, realised that she was tired, too tired to argue or force Devi to do anything. She shrugged and shook her head. Pa shrugged it off too.

"Whatever works for you dear."

After chewing through quite a few moments of silence at the table, Devi looked around, and even though the shroud of tiredness that had fallen upon her, she realised, this was it. The darkness was spreading and it had infiltrated here, her home too. It was contagious. All the Rasas were contagious, like a flu. Except Hasya was a happy flu. When she caught on, everybody in the home was smiling and happy and tinkling like wind chimes. And now, Vibhatsa was here, taking over her spot. Aversion had extended her arms into their home. The swirling gloom of the blue, the complete disinterest, hung there, above their dinner table. Devi realised, it was they who had allowed her in, fed her, made her larger than she needed to be. If only she could sense it, then only she could change it, Devi realised.

In the morning, Devi headed out to draw her *kolam* though she really didn't feel like it. She did just a simple one. Dharmendar didn't like it very much. He thought it was an emoji but actually it was the sun. Devi felt irritable and didn't laugh as much when he cracked a joke about it, something about the sun being gloomy and needing to cheer up. Devi just dragged herself back to Ammamma's room and shut the door. She was right.

Peeli Dhoop was all snowed over, white and pale and bleak like she had never seen it before.

Devi looked at it and felt exhausted, though she had just woken up. She felt angry, cranky, hungry and just not wanting to interact with anyone at all today.

With every remaining ounce of her strength, she folded her hands together in front of her face, and peering deeply into them, chanted:

"Auuuuuuuuuuuummmmmmmmmmm..." she said, a tiny flicker of light appeared on the outline of her palms.

"Karagre vasate Lakshmi"

A gleam of translucent gold hovered over her palms.

"Karamule Saraswati"

Devi gasped as the outline of a butterfly's wings shimmered to life in a gentle silver.

"Karamadhye sthitaha Gauri"

A rose flash from the middle of her palm outwards towards the edges, filling in the contours and details of the butterfly, speckles and dots, lines and veins.

"Prabhate kara darshanam"

Devi's hands fell away into her lap as the familiar silver gold and rose gold butterfly form flapped its wings into life and began to stir into the air. The room sparkled with the flashes emanating from the flutter and streaks of light transformed the swirl around Devi. In an instant she felt her tiredness drop off, her feet return to mobility and the vice-like grip the darkness had been gaining around her heart, fall away.

"Oh, thank god you're back," Devi gasped.

"I'm always here Devi, you just have to work against what's obstructing you sometimes."

"I thought I was fine and I could manage on my own this time you know. I didn't want to keep summoning you. I wanted to prove to you that I was strong. That I could do this."

"Arre, musth elephant. I am a part of you. You are not summoning someone else. It's always okay to ask for help and it's always even more okay to ask yourself for some laughter, wonder and compassion. None of us do anything on our own. We all need each other."

"Great, let's go," said Devi, truly delighted and feeling a warm, loving feeling spreading all over her. "You can tell me all about everything I've missed on the way to the Bhugola."

Hasya looked out of the window and into the sky. It was a gloomy day, clouds gathering in the sky. And it wasn't even the monsoon season.

Even before they had left the house, the sky had burst and the rain had begun to pour. The wind rattled the window of Devi's bedroom.

They skated down a slide of packed snow on a brown sled, a piece of smoothened and well-worn back with handles at the sides to hold on to. It could have been a fun ride if there was a Santa's elf factory or something at the end of it. Just honestly, it wasn't. The landscape was dull and greyish white as far as the eye could see, fields and towns and cities full of it, like a really plain Christmas card. Devi shivered, though Hasya had handed her a warm fleece jacket, no matter how much she pulled at the buttons, the cold still seemed to seep through to her bones. They arrived at a tundra of frozen snow, packed dense into a barren wasteland, where nothing grew.

"Is this the land of Vibhatsa? Devi asked, disbelieving. It was so radically different from the other lands.

Hasya nodded, sadly. It wasn't so much Vibhatsa's land, it was the frozen north of it, a wasteland where she would come to hibernate.

Vibhatsa, the silent one, so lost in herself, the sister who never mingled, was so filled with self-loathing, for herself and others, that the water element in her had frozen solid, rendering her wings unflyable. She rarely went out. She really didn't see the point. She hibernated for the most part. Once in a blue moon, when Vira emerged, she got her new pair of wings from her and went back to sleep.

It wasn't that Vibhatsa was lazy, she found it difficult sometimes to get out of bed. And the thing is when Vibhatsa didn't want to mingle, neither did anyone in her land, so soon, there was nobody there. There were no crowds at the market place, no children in the park, no commuters on the buses. Nobody saw movies or went to concerts or for strolls and balloon rides. There were a few service grey bunnies who kept things running, but even they had pulled up their collars and put on their headphones, which as everyone knew, was the universal sign for not wanting to be disturbed.

Some of those who could still find their courage had migrated and gone off to Vira's land. The moon baths had brought out the orange in some of them. The rest had found their hidey holes and gone to sleep.

The sky in Vibhatsa's land was originally blue but you could barely tell anymore, it was so covered over by blizzards and snowstorms. The climate was hostile and pushed people inwards. Some homes had a small fire going to keep them warm, a gentle orange glow that laboured on, a promise that maybe someday, things would change soon, but it was limited to a small corner of their hearths, and they used all their energy to keep it going.

"It is quite important," Hasya said to Devi, "that whatever happens, you do not go to sleep okay? The blue will try to get into you, it gets into your bones, and into your mind, and when it does, it just sends you straight off to sleep."

"What are we doing? Why are we here? Can't we go somewhere more cheerful. I don't want to be here," Devi protested. She had felt her legs turn to lead before and she didn't want to feel the cold in her bones again. It was a horrible sensation.

"We have to confront the cold. We are searching for Vibhatsa," Hasya said.

"Searching for her? Why do we need to rouse her? Let her be," Devi said, alarmed.

"Because without Vibhatsa, none of us have it in us to overcome Raudra and Bhayanaka," Hasya said.

A blizzard was growling down the street by now. Hasya and Devi slipped into a café that sold hot white chocolate to keep themselves warm. They thanked the lumbering polar bear at the counter who passed it to them and waved them to a table by the fire. He just grunted in response and disappeared.

"I don't understand how all this works," Devi said.

"You forget, we sisters have a bit of each other in ourselves. It may seem like it's best to leave Vibhatsa alone, but the thing is, she really is the most vital person in our fight. We absolutely have to rouse her from her hibernation," Hasya explained.

Only when we feel sufficiently disgusted with the state of our circumstances can we decide to change them. We have to be fed up with the way things are to want a new way of living and being. We have to really not want to live this way any longer. As long as we're kind of okay with things, we go off to sleep. We live with whatever comes and make a virtue of it.

"How does Vibhatsa not know that? Were you guys not very nice to her?" Devi wanted to know.

"I suppose some of it is my and Adbhuta and Sringara's fault," Hasya admitted. "We allowed her to turn her lens inwards, against herself. You see Devi, too much of any Rasa is bad. There's a good expression of us and a bad expression. The more we rub off on each other, the more we keep each other in balance. I suppose we, the fire and other water butterflies, are more vibrant, and we just didn't notice her slip away. When there's just too much of us, of love, wonder, mirth, and you're kinda blue, you can begin to love the pain too much too. That's when we start wallowing in things," Hasya said.

"Vibhatsa began to enjoy her pain you mean," Devi asked. Hasya nodded.

Devi thought of a boy in her neighbourhood who was always being scolded, Aryan. She could peep into his house from her balcony. And he was always studying, or rushing to class, or crying. There were always loud noises of shouting and screaming coming from his window, sometimes the ominous sounds of whacking too. And Aryan never spoke back. Devi always noticed that she never heard his voice. But in school, Aryan was the naughtiest boy in class, always taking other people's pens and pencils and disturbing them when they were doing something. She hadn't understood it till now. Now she just felt really bad for him.

A silence fell upon the empty cafe. Devi looked around. It was like drinking hot chocolate in someone's cupboard.

There were just boxes and boxes marked 'chocolate' against the walls, many of them not even unpacked. The fire crackled and the two lamps on the wall shone dimly. It was altogether gloomy. From somewhere behind the counter, the polar bear began to gently snore.

"That's because his language of love is Vibhatsa now. When someone's always being told how worthless they are, they think that's the way people will show them love, by showing them how worthless they are, and then they do it to others too," Hasya explained.

"How do you deal with that? It wasn't his fault, that was what he was taught," Devi said.

Hasya agreed. "It wasn't his fault at all. It's what he knows. The trick is not to let Adbhuta or Sringara get too dominant. They're lovely but only in proportion."

"I get it, when you're in another land, don't summon up Sringara or Adbhuta too much, or you'll love it too much. Is that why it's just you and me on this arctic expedition here today?" Devi looked out of the window, it had stopped snowing.

"Yup, they'll always be a bit of them in you. Enough to light a fire and keep yourself warm at it, but..."

"More and you'll actually increase the blue. Who knew? How odd," Devi said.

"You just need enough love of yourself to direct Vibhatsa outwards, at the things and people that make you feel bad about yourself," Hasya explained. Then, you could move to another land. Don't build a house in your sorrows, as

Ammamma would say, but do visit them once in a while. Too many people were building houses in the tundras of their existence. Nobody wanted to live in the north pole, they just wanted the presents that came from it.

"Come on let's go find Vibhatsa now, before it starts up again," Hasya said.

"I still don't get why we need her," Devi replied, really not wanting to leave the cosy café for the blistering cold.

Yet, even Devi knew that until the self-loathing turned the beings of all the lands against the way they were being treated by Raudra and Bhayanaka, they wouldn't find it in them to rebel. And the beings of Hasya, Adbhuta, Sringara, and Vira were loved and joyful and wonderstruck. They had nothing to look at with disgust. Because Vibhatsa had gone to sleep for a long dark winter, they didn't have a trace of aversion awake in them just now. They felt compassion for all the refugees, but no disgust for Raudra and Bhayanaka who were causing them to flee. And without Vibhatsa, they would never get round to fighting them. Yes, it was imperative that Devi and Hasya find Vibhatsa and rouse her.

"Ready?" Hasya asked.

"Oh, gosh! How do we do this?" Devi asked.

"I have a plan, follow me," Hasya said, as she opened the door and flew out into the snow packed streets towards the centre of the town plaza.

The streets were deserted, the beings were all in their homes. Here and there, Devi spotted the gentle glow of fire, straining itself to survive against the weather.

Devi couldn't understand what they were doing. Would they go house to house, rousing people until they found Vibhatsa? Did Vibhatsa even live in a house?

"Okay, start," Hasya said, when they had reached the middle. Though middle of what Devi could not make out, it all looked very much the same.

"Start what?"

"Tell me a *vidukathai*."

"That's the plan? Are you crazy? In this storm? You've lost it. I'm leaving," Devi said.

But of course, she didn't know how to go back on her own though she said 'Elumicham pazham' a couple of times out loud. Then she gave up and just marched back to Hasya. It was too cold to throw a tantrum here. Easier to comply.

"Trust me on this. Just tell me a *vidukathai*. The funniest one you've got," Hasya said.

Devi thought this was all a bit batty but decided to go with it anyway, since she didn't really see a choice here.

She thought for a little while.

"I weigh nothing, but you can still see me. I can make anything lighter. What am I?"

Hasya couldn't answer, but Devi suspected she was faking it. After all, she could read her mind. But that was a skill Hasya seemed to switch on and off, depending on when she needed to use it.

"A hole," Devi said.

Hasya chuckled. It was only when she cracked a smile that Devi realised Hasya hadn't been herself throughout this trip.

She had gotten all serious and gone a bit blue herself. It was nice to see her smile again; warming somehow. Her tingling wings sent out a shower of sparkles that lit up the frigid air.

Devi summoned up another one.

"You measure my life in hours and I serve you by expiring. I'm quick when I'm thin and slow when I'm fat. The wind is my enemy."

Hasya tried a couple of answers, but nothing struck home. "Umbrella?" "Time?"

"A candle!" Devi said.

Hasya started to laugh. Encouraged, Devi pulled out another one. This was an original, inspired by her ordeal every time she came home from that exhausting rollerblading class.

"When do you go in through one hole and come out through two holes at the same time?" Devi asked. Hasya hadn't a clue.

"When you're putting on trousers."

Hasya laughed and laughed at this one. Soon both of them were collapsing in laughter. The warmth encircled them and began to warm them up a bit on the inside. And that made more and more jokes come out. And truth be told, Devi didn't think these were that funny. But here's the thing about mirth, sometimes when you laugh, it can catch on and the joke can begin to run away with itself.

"A man on a soccer field kicked a ball away. The ball came back at once at the same speed. No one else and no object directed it back. How?" Devi asked.

Hasya shrugged. A small crowd of beings was starting to gather around them now. The Polar Bear café manager, who had woken up from his nap. A bunny tram driver. The station master who was so white a cat, you could only see his deep blue eyes blinking in the snow. A couple of doves and some white mice. "He kicked the ball up in the air."

By now the whole crowd began to join Hasya. Soon everybody was laughing and chuckling and slapping their knees and harrumphing. Devi felt like a stand-up comic doing open mic in a quite odd theatre.

Devi couldn't help it, she began to laugh as she spoke too. Soon she was wiping tears of laughter from her eyes and trying hard to speak without guffawing.

Hasya's chimes got louder and louder. It began to reverberate through the town like bells; at first little ones and then great big ones. Sparkles lit up the streets and went up to windows. Gold and silver and rose starlight began to stream down the streets. Devi could see the town around wake up and transform. She kept going.

"Who lives an exhausting life?"

"An exhaust fan!"

"What can answer in any language? What can speak without a mouth? What can sing without an ear?" "An echo!"

"What's as big as an elephant but doesn't weigh anything at all?"

"The elephant's shadow!"

There was a small crowd around them holding their tummies and kicking their legs in the air. The sun had come out now and while the snow remained piled up by the sides of the street, the air was a little bit lighter and not quite so bone-chilling. The wind had died down, and the sounds of beings stirring, happy banter, catching the tram, switching on some music, began to filter through the town. The more beings saw others get out and about, the more they wanted to too.

As the snow storm ceased, Adbhuta, Sringara, and Vira came flying down and began to sprinkle the streets with their love and wonder. Green shoots began to burst out of the dead flower boxes in the windows and in the once grassy lawns. Evergreens shed their burdens of snow and shook out their leaves, perfuming the air with pine.

And Devi kept going.

"Why shouldn't you write with a broken pencil?"

"Because it's pointless!"

"Why did the scarecrow win an award?" "He was outstanding in his field!"

At first it was tough, but then every riddle she had ever heard started to flow like a river of mirth, and Hasya took it over from there.

Suddenly there was a pale rustling, the sound of a mournful horn, and Vibhatsa appeared.

She had been awakened from her slumber.

"What. Is. Going. ON?" she asked, annoyed and irritated.

The crowd of beings dispersed.

"Hasya, Sringara, Adbhuta, why are you interfering in my land. Can't I even be left alone? Nobody has any respect for me. I told you I don't want to see you. Am I that insignificant to you that you won't even respect my wishes?" Vibhatsa said.

Devi could tell she was feeling extremely attacked by this invasion into her space.

Vibhatsa began to weep.

"NO!" Hasya thundered.

Everyone looked at her, startled, including Vibhatsa and Adbhuta.

"Wow that was wonderful," Adbhuta whispered. Devi tried not to giggle.

"If you start crying again Vibhatsa, it will start snowing again. Please. NO. I won't let you do it."

"And we need you," Devi said.

Vibhatsa looked confused. "Need me? Nobody needs me. Beings shun me, and rightly too."

"Well, we do. We absolutely cannot fight this battle without you," Vira said.

Vibhatsa looked down and away. "Whatever it is I can't do it. You know I can't do it Vira. You're the one with all the courage, you do it."

"It's not your courage we need Vibhatsa, it's your loathing," Vira said.

Vibhatsa looked up, surprised. "My loathing? That is everything that is wrong in me. I don't understand. How can any of what I am be useful? I thought my only use was to allow you to get past me and lead you to courage."

"I'm sorry we have allowed you to feel this way and not shown up for you sooner. But truth is, in some circumstances, you are exactly what we need," Sringara said, kindly.

"You are the only Rasa who can stop the hate Vibhatsa," Vira said.

"Me? How? Surely you're mistaken," Vibhatsa replied.

"Direct your loathing outwards, Vibhatsa, away from yourself."

Vibhatsa clutched herself and shuddered. "I knew it, you've come to take everything I have away from me," she said. "It's all I have and now you want me to give it away? What will I be left with? I'll be naked, exposed," she cried out. Vibhatsa couldn't see any way in which she could help others.

"We are here. We will help you now," Hasya began.

"Devi, tell me a riddle about other people, please. People who do bad things," Hasya said to Devi. This time Devi knew better than to argue. She had to think a bit, she didn't know so many jokes about really bad people, but she managed two really good ones.

"Two cannibals are chewing a clown. One says to the other: 'Hey, does it taste kinda funny to you?'"

"What is greater than God, more evil than the Devil, rich people need it, poor people have it and if you eat it you'll die?"

"What?" Vibhatsa asked.

"Nothing," Devi shrugged.

At first, Vibhatsa didn't understand. But then, she began to slowly smile.

"I see what you're trying to tell me. I can laugh at other people, at evil people, at the people who do bad in the world. I can ridicule them, and see them with loathing."

"Exactly. I'm asking you to use me to channel your disgust instead of directing it at yourself," Hasya said.

"But...but...won't that make them angry?" Vibhatsa asked, concerned. "Won't they look at me with disgust then?"

"The antidote to disgust is disgust, Vibhatsa, so the antidote to that which is directed at you is yours directed at them," Vira said.

"You're asking me to fight back," Vibhatsa said, understanding.

Adbhuta put a wing around her sister. "I'm sorry I neglected you. I'm sorry we all did. You must have felt so devalued. You are not at all someone to be avoided. You are rare and beautiful and serve a divine purpose. We can call it discerning. You can set the standard to which we all operate."

Vira presented Vibhatsa with her very own suit of armour, a breast plate and a helmet with her own insignia engraved onto it.

"What is all this?" Vibhatsa asked. "I'm no soldier. I don't know how to fight for myself let alone others."

"Nonsense, of course you are," Vira replied. "When you direct yourself towards those who don't treat you right, it protects you. When you direct your expression towards those who harm others, it protects the innocent."

Vibhatsa had never thought of herself in that way. She was a suit of armour. Or at any rate, she could be one.

Devi stepped up. "You can do this Vibhatsa. I know so many of my friends who get bullied or called names, and they think something is wrong with them, and that's why they're suffering. You can help them express their aversion to the people who harm them instead of towards themselves. They need you to do that for them."

Vibhatsa nodded. She saw now, why it was necessary for her to act. "I can do that, Devi."

Adbhuta held Vibhatsa's wing in her own and focussed. Some yellow passed from her into her sister. A small yellow glow lit up Vibhatsa's heart and eyes, warming her from the inside. Sringara stepped up next and took Vibhatsa's other wing. Vira stood next to her and Hasya completed the circle, taking Adbhuta's hand in her own. As they formed a circle, the colours began to radiate bands of colours that went equally through them all. Adbhuta's sunny yellow, Vibhatsa's pale icy blue, Sringara's sapling green, Vira's saffron and Hasya's white. Round and round the circle spun until the colours had infused them all, and they shone with the sparkles of each other's lustre alongside their own. Vibhatsa's wings shone with the depth of the night sky, a midnight blue speckled with tiny pin points of a thousand stars.

As the combined light of the butterflies ascended on the land, the snow melted, and spring began to resound. Birds chirped, the sun beamed and Chika appeared, with his stethoscope and army of chameleon tree doctors, to check on the sprigs emerging from the melting snow.

"Yup, it's ok. We have a heartbeat. We can save them!" he shouted.

A great cheer rung out from the beings of Vibhatsa. Slowly they began to shuffle down the streets. The markets flung open, beings brought out their preserved bottles of elderberry cider, the smell of blackcurrant pie wafted into the air, somewhere some light jazz came on and a store that sold blue cheese pizza upped its shutters and began to fill the street with the fragrance of yeast. It would be some time before the town would get back to normal, but after a really long time, Vibhatsa was awake again. Which meant they had a voice, they mattered, someone somewhere cared. And for now, that was motivation enough.

Vibhatsa shuffled uncomfortably.

So much interference.

Vira spotted it and hugged her twin. "We know you're uncomfortable Vibhatsa and we're sorry, but we've decided that we cannot leave you alone any longer. We are a part of your life whether you want it or not, and you can express yourself without judgement as long as we're around."

Devi nodded. "We're your safe space," she said.

Vibhatsa looked at her feet. "Raudra always allowed me to express myself with her," she said. "She used to say venting is good."

"Yes it is. We know you love Raudra, we love her too. Sometimes we forget our way when we're not there for each other, when we get lost in our worlds and forget how deeply connected we all are. It's a mistake we've all made. But we are here now, pulling each other back from the brink. We want you to know we love you too and we're here for you," Sringara said.

Vibhatsa shook out her freshly awakened glistening night sky wings and felt a deep sense of satisfaction, something she hadn't felt in a really long time.

They went and each got a slice of pizza, pungent and aromatic with acai berries and blue tomatoes on it, glasses of blue corn juice and sat down in the gazebo at the park, next to the lily pond where blue ducks were just beginning to flock back to their freshly gushing habitat.

"Fill me in," Vibhatsa said. "What have I missed while I've been asleep?"

This was the tough part. Vibhatsa was the only sister who didn't know.

They told her as gently as they could, but it broke Vibhatsa's heart anyway to hear that beloved gentle Shanta was trapped in the fire. She felt betrayed by what Raudra and Bhayanaka had done. But also, she felt aversion towards their actions. She understood why her sisters had come to wake her. What they were doing had to be stopped.

She turned to Hasya, "Tell me, what can I do to help?"

Hasya smiled. "We need you to rouse aversion in our lands."

Vibhatsa looked horrified. "Are you sure? Most people keep me away from them, to spread this among the lands..."

she trailed off and gestured towards the streets of the town that were only just limping back to life. "You don't want your lands turning into this," she said sadly.

Hasya embraced her. "They won't. And stop worrying about your own either. None of them will anymore. Until now, we lived and worked in silos. We didn't know either, how important it was for each of us to carry a little bit of the other in our hearts."

Thanks to Devi's arrival, the Rasa sisters could all be present at the same time, cross their boundaries, intermingle and connect in ways that they hadn't ever before. And the more they did so, the more they began to know their strengths, both on their own and together.

Vibhatsa nodded and stood up.

The sisters held hands and set off. Sringara, Adbhuta, Hasya, and Vira with Vibhatsa in the middle. As Devi stood in the park and watched, the sisters flew across all the lands, over the impenetrable mountain ranges and across the sparkling oceans, sketching a beautiful semi-rainbow, a Meghadhanush, one like no one had ever seen, across the sky of the Rasa Bhugola.

It was a promise that they would be united, that they would fight the darkness, and in the end, the rainbow would also be complete.

When all the butterfly dust had been carried by the wind, settling evenly across the Bhugola, the beings woke out of their blissful bubbles and saw the smoke rising from Shanta's land; and they knew that things were not okay. They were disgusted at all that was disturbing their peace and vowed to do something about it.

Sringara, Adbhuta, and Hasya flew back to their lands to mobilise the forces and to announce that Vira had begun recruitment and training for the army that would march against Raudra and Bhayanaka.

Chapter 6

The Loneliest Man in the World

Devi couldn't return to the Rasa Bhugola for a while. She had her mid-term exams coming up and Mom had really started focussing on the whole 'classes' thing. Devi had at first let it pass thinking it was one of those phases grown-ups go through. You know, when sometimes parents feel the need to do things, and feel the need to make kids do things, because they feel guilty for not doing enough for them, or for being busy in their own lives. The outcome is either gifts, which is always preferable, or 'the guilt plan' as Devi called it.

The guilt plan was an extreme form of structuring a child's day. It was akin to an Olympic sport. There would be timetables and lists and schedules, and running from here to there and there to here, until everyone was too exhausted for what the grown-ups referred to as 'get up to mischief'. And you know what that meant, no time to day dream or think or explore how they really really felt about things. Mostly, because grown-ups couldn't bear to sit down and contemplate how they really felt about things, otherwise they might look at the reality of their lives and not go farther. Parents, Devi noticed, often did these things to themselves too. While contemplations like these never quite occurred to Devi earlier, now, having dived deep into the world of the Rasa Bhugola, she thought about all the wonderful sights and sounds and colours that her parents seemed to be missing out on, and that she would have missed out on if Hasya hadn't come to find her.

"Your life must be just a blur of colour, mustn't it?" Devi asked Mom one morning, while eating breakfast.

Mom, who had a piece of toast in her mouth while she was brushing her hair while attempting to shove the laundry into the machine, and taking something that was beginning to burn off the stove at the same time, managed to shrug.

"Waffumean?"

"I mean, when was the last time you had time you know?"

Mom threw her head back and laughed, choking on a bit of the toast a little.

"I don't want time, I'm happy running around, lots to do, being productive is good."

"You look a little all over the place to me," is what Devi really wanted to say, but instead she went with: "Yeah, yeah I get all that but is it the only good? Do you know Sayed Haider Raza's 'Le Mer' mom?"

"Le what?"

"Imagine you were swimming in it..."

"In what more? I'm already swimming in it!"

"...a bluish-purple sea Mom, keep up, and dolphins come up to ferry you to the beach, where you bathed by moonlight, and found your courage, and acquired your warm glow of saffron in your heart, what would your life be like then?"

Mom, despite everything she had to get done before work, put everything down and managed to stare at Devi for a moment like she had lost her marbles.

"Have they been teaching you art in school again?"

Devi nodded, mostly to avoid further questions.

"What I mean is, if you had the time to explore, what would you do?"

Mom realised Devi was being serious.

"I'm so sorry Devi, I know I've been a bit rushed, that's a great question, but you know, right now, off the top of my head, honestly, I'd just sleep. The sleep of babies. I'd sleep for hours and hours and hours."

"...and would you dream?"

Mom took a moment and sat down at the table.

"Yes, I'd dream of a little house in the hills facing the Himalayan peaks, a place of..."

"Shanta. Tranquillity," Devi interrupted, as though she knew.

Mom looked at her.

"Why yes," she said quietly, seriously. "Tranquillity, peace."

"And once you had it in the core of you, wouldn't you do anything in the world to protect it?"

Mom nodded.

"What if you already had it but you weren't protecting it, and were letting it melt?"

"Is this another of your *vidukathais* Devi?"

Devi shrugged now.

"Gotta go mom, I've got drawing class now," she said hopping off her stool, grabbing her bag and heading out the door.

More than fifteen days had passed since Devi had returned to the Bhugola. The more Devi threw herself into her classes, the less time she had to think about the Bhugola, until it just seemed a distant dream, some place you visit on vacation, a picnic spot. And the less she thought about it, the less urgent its requirements felt. Devi was falling into that trap that the grown-ups were laying for children, making them more and more like themselves, so they could be less and less like themselves.

Devi had made new friends, she was laughing and chattering and exchanging stories. She was drawing her *kolams* every morning and was getting better at it. She had more and more followers on Instagram and even got mentioned in a small local newspaper weekend write-up as the '*kolam* kid'. People she didn't even know kept sending her new designs to try on Instagram. She had a birthday coming up. She had a lot of reading to keep up with for school projects and between rollerblading, karate, and dance classes, she had plenty of expression that was expected of her and very little time to think about what she was expressing.

Devi kept going and going until one morning she woke up and realised she really didn't feel anything anymore.

There were warning signs. She should have known. She should have seen the Great Meltdown of 2022 coming.

Pa and Mom and she had been out for a movie. Pa asked her a simple enough question: how she felt about it.

Devi, who was eating an ice cream, shrugged.

"What does that mean, Devi?" asked Pa, a little annoyed, he couldn't tell why.

"I don't really know, Pa. Try as I might, I can't seem to think of anything that comes up."

"Did you find it funny, sad, boring?"

"Ugh, these questions are just so boring, Pa," Devi said, suddenly annoyed. "I just don't know, Pa. I just don't feel anything at all about it," she said. What she really meant to say was, "I don't feel like investigating my feelings at this time because all the doing keeps me from having to," and promptly was distracted by a window display at the mall which had shiny green ballet shoes, the kind she had no need for but plenty of want for, on sale. That was not the problem that would lead to the Great Meltdown of 2022, as Devi would forever after refer to it. What happened next did.

"That's so funny," Pa thought, as he watched her go, "that's exactly how I feel: nothing."

And Pa sat with this thought, wondering what he really felt, until it occurred to him that it was probably necessary to feel something, anything at all.

He looked at Devi, running around the food court, wondering what to order. She seemed happy but he didn't want her to feel nothing either.

Then, it occurred to him, the thought that many parents rarely admit to themselves, he didn't want his kid to grow up to be just like him. He wanted her to grow up to be better.

He had to stop her, Pa realised, from turning into mini-me. And that's what both he and Mom were doing.

Feeling nothing, it occurred to Pa, was something that people did when they couldn't bear to feel what they felt. And that's when they began to *do* everything, more and more. To avoid feeling something. And he felt a snowy cold begin to settle in his heart.

As he sat there, Pa began to feel a sense of disgust for himself, for his life, and for everything around him. As he sat there, and mulled how far he had come from the life he really wanted to live, he did something he had wanted to do for a really long time. He picked up his phone and dialled his boss.

"I won't be coming to work for a week or so. I need some time off."

"A week?" said his boss, alarmed. "Are you alright? You've never taken a week off before."

"I know, which is why I need it now," Pa said to him.

"You have to plan these things, Sanjay, you just can't take so much time off at the last minute. What about all the dues and deliverables, you simply have to come in," the boss said.

"I'll work from home for a few days until you can get things in order but you're going to have to excuse me," Pa said. He was firm.

"But why, tell me why."

"I'm... well, unwell."

"Unwell? You sound perfectly fine to me."

"It's not... that kind of not feeling well," Pa said.

"Then what kind is it Sanjay? This sounds like an excuse to me."

"I can't explain it boss, I just don't feel like I can keep going," Pa said. They argued for a while but in the end the boss realised there really was nothing he could do. Pa was simply not going to come in to work.

Pa looked around, satisfied with himself, and beamed.

Devi, who had returned with an ice cream cone in her hand and a couple of burgers and cheesy fries, overheard her father's side of the conversation, but didn't say anything.

Mom walked up behind her. She asked Pa, "What's up? Who was that on the phone?"

"The boss. I'm taking a few days off, Neela."

"What? Why? Was there a wedding we had to attend I have forgotten about?"

Pa smiled. He was so tired of constantly having to go somewhere and do something. "No, we aren't going anywhere. Just... I feel like it," Pa said.

"Whoa," said Devi. Even she knew that wasn't something you just said to Mom. Mom never did anything because she just felt like it. Fireworks!

Mom raised her eyebrows at Pa but said nothing just then. It was a tense ride home.

It was time for a class again in a few hours, and then one more and then one more. At the scheduled time of departure for the eight o' clock Coding for Girls class, Devi refused to go.

No matter what Mom said, she simply wouldn't go downstairs to Sashi aunty's session in the club house and join in.

Mom, who was already mad at Pa, began to scold her.

Devi, usually a docile child, who could already sense the tension in the room, snapped, and began to shout back.

"And I told you I cannot do this anymore!"

She began to throw things around the house until Pa hugged her to restrain her.

And then for a very long time, Pa and Devi hugged each other, and she cried.

That night, there was a huge row.

Devi heard it lying in bed and staring at the ceiling. It was at times like this she wished she had a brother or a sister.

"I blame you for this, Sanjay, with your own irresponsible behaviour. Now she also thinks it's perfectly fine to bunk her classes and do whatever she wants to. You just can't stop doing things because you simply don't feel like doing them anymore. What example is that setting for Devi? Think!" Mom was saying.

"Maybe I absolutely did think about that. Maybe I don't want her to be like me," Pa said.

"Why, what's wrong with you? Or are you saying you don't want her to be like me?"

Oops, dangerous territory. Don't answer that, don't answer that, Devi was thinking.

"For god's sake it's only a few days off," Pa replied instead. Neat save.

"With no good reason. What if they fire you for this or don't give you your promotion?"

"We'll be fine," Pa said, nonchalantly. Devi knew it was the nonchalance that always got Mom's goat.

"But what example are you setting, just when we are getting her to run around and be productive."

"*You*, you mean."

"What?"

"*You* are getting her to run around and be productive, as if that was all that mattered."

"Don't you dare turn this around on me, you can see she's been doing well lately."

"Is that what we think of as doing well now, Neela; not having time to do anything but well?"

"That's how we've always done things, the more productive you are the better you are coping."

"Now you see why I took leave."

"I don't understand you."

"Maybe it's time we changed the way we did things here."

"Get real Sanjay, that's not how the world works. These ideas you have they are nebulous things; they are not real. Nothing in the mind is real, you can just push past it all. You just have to be determined to. You lack discipline. Go to the gym or for a walk or something. You'll feel better."

"What if I don't want to? What if I can't anymore?"

"Maybe you don't feel like it, but it's how we need to work. We need to build our own world."

"What kind of world is this? Living in silos, in this way?"

As she heard her Pa make space for his mind, Devi knew what her father was saying was true. She knew the mind was real, those mountains were real, those veins of black trying to take over were real, the blizzard and the snow storm that shut everything down were real. Those who thought the mind was some nebulous thing only needed to struggle against its resistance; the runner who just can't make his legs go, the painter whose fingers won't frame the image, the way Devi struggled with her petals sometimes, the writer pushing past the mental block, or like them, Mom, when she just didn't feel like cooking, and Pa, who just didn't feel like going to work another day, or others like her, the student who simply couldn't take another class. To people like us, Devi thought, we already know the mind can be a mountain that just won't budge from our path.

Devi saw it clearly now. The Rasa Bhugola, her own, not Ammamma's, not Pa's, not Mom's, not anyone else's. She had been avoiding it, trying so hard to dismiss it all as a dream, a chimera, some flight of fantasy, but it was real. It was as real as it could be. And those who didn't recognise it as real were inviting themselves into the shut-down of a deep hibernating loneliness, cut off not so much from the world, as from themselves. Pa was already on his way there, Devi realised. She recognised the signs by now.

"It is better than being the loneliest man in the world," Pa was saying to Mom, when Devi burst out of her room, and hugged him.

She wouldn't let her father disappear into the icy wilderness of Vibhatsa.

Mom and Pa stopped arguing at once. They tried to console her. "You shouldn't have heard all of that, Devi. We're sorry we scared you, Devi. It's okay. We're fine. We're not arguing," Pa said.

As things quietened down at home, all at once, they heard a commotion rise all around the colony. A great number of voices clamouring from all directions. They ran to the balcony. In all the homes, children were throwing things, couples were arguing, those who were working had quit their jobs, parents were angry and Moms were rebellious. A great quarrel rose up in home after home, flat after flat. As people noticed others were listening to them, they shut their doors and windows and pulled the curtains to dull the noise. Devi could see the blue glow of their televisions and the LED bulbs. Outside, it began to rain, and there was an unusual hailstorm. A chilly

wind brewed. Then suddenly, the house began to tremble and sway. It lasted a few seconds. Then it was all quiet again.

"Earthquake? Hailstorm in Mumbai? What is happening?" Mom said, running to put on the channel news.

"Come away from the window," she said, taking Devi in to the living room. Pa shut all the doors and windows behind them.

Devi looked upon the all too familiar scene, the great shut in was beginning, and she felt a shudder, her feet began to turn to lead and she felt a heaviness inside. She knew what was coming. The unthinkable had happened.

Vibhatṣa, Raudra, and Bhayanaka had joined forces.

And they were coming for the world.

Chapter 7

Shoot the Messenger

Devi waited until the early hours of the morning, when Pa and Mom had fallen asleep. The clamour of the hail against window panes and thudding into balconies had ceased, and the unseasonal lightning strikes and thunderstorm had passed. On the news, they were calling it the climate change event of the century; a hurricane was lurching towards Mumbai, expected to bring high winds and raging floods. There had been tremors, indicating that what the news channels called 'The Big One', was inevitable. Mom said it was lucky they were on the higher floors; they would be safe. Simultaneously, forest fires were breaking out in otherwise verdant thickets. Glaciers that had stood for centuries were beginning to thaw, causing rivers to run more swollen and flood the plains. Scientists were beginning to see the rise of diseases, plagues, viruses, hitherto unknown. Mom switched off the news, it was too depressing to watch, and cuddled Devi, comforting her, though Devi could tell it was Mom who needed comforting. She didn't know what was going on in her stable and secure world. Pa had gone to bed, drawing the blanket up to his neck though it wasn't really all that cold. He didn't plan to leave it for days. He just wanted to sleep he said. He just wanted to be left alone. Mom as always, found her courage by throwing herself into more work. She cleaned out cupboards that were already clean, and organised shelves that were already organised and took on more work appointments for the next day than she usually would have.

"You know Pa's not feeling well, Devi. I need you to be the mature one, okay? Just do your own stuff, your chores, your school work, be focussed. We can get through this," Mom said, ruffling her hair and kissing her on the forehead, as she tucked her into bed that night.

Devi looked at her with disappointment in her eyes. Mom still didn't get it.

She couldn't blame her; she hadn't got it herself for a very long time. The more you turned to structure, order, to the strict lists of things to do, the more you set the boundaries between the Rasas, the more you isolated them from each other, and Vibhatsa, Bhayanaka and Raudra were strengthened. When the Rasas couldn't communicate with each other, misunderstanding bred between them and they were unable to work together. It was up to her now. She knew what to do. She just had to get there.

It was around 3 a.m., Devi heard the clock in the kitchen chime, when Mom had stopped her tossing and turning. Devi slipped into Ammamma's room. In the dark she couldn't see the painting and she didn't want to switch on the light and wake anyone. But wasn't it supposed to glow?

"Elumicham pazham," she said, urgently. Nothing happened.

"Elumicham pazham," she said, loudly.

Wind chimes tinkled. "What are you doing? Are you trying to have a conversation with the painting?" a familiar voice said.

"Hasya!" Devi loud-whispered.

"Shhhhhh... you'll wake... you know..."

"Why didn't you come sooner?"

"Well, you took your time conjuring me, didn't you?" Hasya whispered back.

"What conjuring? You pretty much come and go as you please it seems," Devi annoyed-whispered back.

"No, I don't. You have to want me around or I can't come," Hasya indignantly-whispered back.

"Fine time to tell me, isn't it?" Devi fury-whispered back. "Can you switch your stuff on please? We don't have much time."

cough *cough* *cough* Hasya said.

"I've to save Pa, come on then," Devi urged.

"Ahem ahem," Hasya said.

"Oh right!" Devi said. She'd forgotten, again.

She sighed, sat down, folded her legs and looked at her palms.

"Auuuuummmm
Karagre vasate Lakshmi
Karamadhye Saraswati
Karamule sthitaha Gauri
Prabhate kara darshanam..."

Devi chanted.

Even though she was whispering and in the dark, the familiar words of the chant seemed to rise from the depths of her, as though powered by something far stronger than any fear she was feeling. She felt energised and centred.

"Come on then," she said, as Hasya burst into the being – silver and gold and rose gold, starlight and sparkle flashing through the room, all the brighter in the silence of the night. Thankfully, no one stirred. They rushed towards the painting.

How strange, Devi thought. It wasn't because of the light. She could see it clearly now by the glow of Hasya's wings. It was all dark. Like a blank black sheet. Lightless, contourless, as though there had never been anything there.

"Elumicham pazham," Devi said, nevertheless, ignoring the sinking feeling.

For a little while Devi thought that nothing had happened at all. There was no swoop and no tumble, no thrust and no fall, no figures and beings and images lining her passage. Just a continuous and seamless darkness. And then, as her eyes adjusted to the darkness, and light outlines of black silhouettes came into being, she understood. She was there. They were in the Rasa Bhugola. And it was completely and utterly pitch black now.

"Are we in Bhayanaka's land?" Devi whispered to the only being in the land that was glowing with any form of light, a creeping dread rising upon her even before she heard the answer.

Hasya whispered back: "It's all Bhayanaka's land now."

Devi's heart sank to her stomach.

Hasya turned down her twinkle and sparkle as best she could, retaining a dim outline by which they could at least see where they were headed.

"Where are we going?" Devi whispered.

Hasya pointed, though Devi couldn't quite see in which direction she was pointing. This was the problem with the creeping darkness, once it sheathed everything, you couldn't even see enough to switch on a light. You just ended up groping your way and hoping one came along. It was only people who stood outside the darkness who thought these were easy and obvious things; to switch on a light, find a guide, get to help. When you were in it though, even the simplest of steps became complicated and life threatening, looming like a hazard you haven't even imagined yet.

In the distance, the direction Hasya had been pointing in, was the outline of the Tourmaline range. Somewhere high up, in the heart of it, in the blackest of black canyons where even light was converted to dark, Vira had established camp. Devi looked, to search for any speck of light, that familiar dull orange glow, a small bonfire, anything. But there was nothing. Devi had no clue how on Earth they would get there.

They stumbled along until Devi grabbed Hasya's wing.

"I know, let's head for the river. That courses through all the lands, doesn't it?"

"Yes, but it would take ages to go down all of it, and who knows what dangerous territory it may pass through," Hasya whispered back.

"Right now, it's our only go," Devi whispered back again.

They had to get to camp and get everybody together, that was the only way out of this. Passing through all the lands was just what they needed, however long it took. Adbhuta and Sringara or Vira's soldiers would come and find them. They just had to hope for the best, and besides, the river, being Shanta's melting heart, was another unseen ally. They were safe with her.

The river sparkled silver and white in the distance as it always did, serene and tranquil in its meandering, but both Devi and Hasya, even at this distance, could tell it had swollen up to twice its normal size. Hasya caught hold of Devi by the arm, set to fly, and fluttered her wings. A tiny chime of bells arose and Devi was gripped with fear that they would be found out. With the springing up of fear, her feet felt as heavy as lead, and both Hasya and Devi lurched downwards, plummeting to the Earth.

"Ouch!" Devi groaned, "I forgot. Bhayanaka equals fear equals lead legs. This is no good."

"We'll just have to walk," Hasya said, dusting off her wings.

They started off again towards what seemed like the river. They walked in silence lest they be heard and captured. It seemed an interminable distance, and soon, they realised, whichever way they went, the river seemed to swerve away from them.

It wasn't the river, it was a decoy.

"Now what do we do?" Devi whispered to Hasya. "We can't trust anything in this land."

"That's what they want you to think," said a familiar voice.

"Chaki? Is that you?"

There was a rustle of leaves in the darkness.

Chaki appeared on a tree by the side of the road, nodding at nobody in particular since they couldn't anyway see him. They could just make out an outline.

"Chaki! I could hug you," Devi squealed. Hasya tinkled softly with joy, trying her best not to send out her starlight.

"Please don't, you'd crumple my scarf and it's very hard to keep it nice and crisp," he said, arranging it around his neck. "And with all this dark and blue and fury, we're just having terrible weather. Can't afford to have that happen," he said.

"What is it they want us to think, Chaki?"

"That you can't trust the river, of course. Or the direction, or the wind, or even yourselves and each other," Chaki said, in that bored voice which sounded like he was so tired of telling everyone this and why didn't they just see through the whole charade themselves and save people the time, you know. He needed the sunlight back up for his trees which were beginning to run awfully low on chlorophyll. It was sending the Earth into a horrible tailspin. And these beings were just dawdling around not even able to find themselves a path to the river for god's sake, how would they ever win a war!

But Chaki kept mum and just nodded.

"Of course! Why didn't I think of that!" Hasya cried.

"For someone who is so very bright, you're not very um... well... bright, are you my dear?" Chaki drawled.

Hasya giggled.

"The turtle taxis are waiting for you by the river landing. Just go straight and take a left at the praying mantis's store. He's going to keep rubbing his front legs together until you get there so just follow the noise," Chaki said.

"We're in Sringara's land then?" Devi asked.

Chaki nodded though they couldn't see him, but they could sense him agree. Something sarcastic would have been flung their way if he didn't.

"...But the Cosmos tree?" Devi asked. "Is it safe?"

"Nothing, my dear," Chaki said, ominously, "is safe, and that's not fear, that's the truth."

Devi's heart sank to the bottom of her toes now.

"We absolutely need the lights back on. Be a dear and fix it," Chaki said, turning away. He had work to do in the forests. They could make out from the rustles in the branches that he had gone.

They listened keenly, distinguishing between the noises of the night from the sound that would guide them to safe passage. Ah, there it was, the rubbing.

Devi had never been inside this much of darkness before, she thought, as they followed it. The rhythmic sound unfurled like a thread before them, becoming louder and louder as they followed it.

The praying mantis ushered them in the direction of the landing from there. As they got closer, they heard the sound of water lapping against the bank, and no sooner did they turn the corner than there it was, hidden by the bending boughs of trees conspiratorially bending across her to keep her safe, to minimise disturbance, and reduce the evaporation off her silvery surface.

"If they found her, they could easily trace the Cosmos tree and we wouldn't want that," the praying mantis said.

Shanta was still alive! And so was the Cosmos tree, hidden in the folds of the Peridot.

The turtle taxi whistled at them so they could find him, and slid to the river bank so they could step gingerly on.

"They're all waiting for you, ma'am," the turtle taxi said. "Hold tight."

"Waiting where?" Hasya said.

"In the Tourmaline caves, right turtle taxi?" Devi said.

The turtle taxi nodded.

Hasya turned to look at Devi in surprise. Perhaps Devi didn't note it, but it was the first time Devi had offered a direction that Hasya had asked for. Hasya said nothing. Devi was no longer a visitor to the Bhugola. Despite the darkness, Devi had begun to know the lay of the land. They held on as the turtle taxis slid into the deeper waters and flowed with the current.

As they pushed out, Devi was struck with the mesmerising reflection of the eddying swirls of darkness overhead on the surface of the river. The hypnotic ripples reminded her she was afraid of deep pools, as they expanded to the river's edge. They tauntingly invited her in. Devi shook her head to free her eyes of the gaze. She reminded herself, this was what Bhayanaka did: She reminded you of everything you were afraid of.

She looked back at the flowing waters. One by one, the things that Devi was most afraid of were reflected in it. Monsters from the books she'd read, grade papers with really poor marks, the funerals of the people she loved, being lost in the marketplace and not being able to find her Mom, the face of Ammamma calling to her needing help.

Devi watched them as they appeared, and realised she was not afraid of them anymore. She had just received so much love and so much affection all through her life, especially here in Sringara's land, that their voices sounded louder than that of the dark. The darkness no longer had hold on her here. It was not that Devi did not see the darkness, or feel its presence in her heart, be gripped by fear and overcome by terror. It was that despite it, Devi could keep going. She could watch the fear swell and move past it. It reminded her of what Vira had said about Vibhatsa, that you had to get through the blue to the heart of the saffron. Well, you had to get past the dark to get to the light.

No sooner did Devi realise this, than the film of darkness lifted and the river returned to its silvery white original state. They begin to flow towards the Tourmaline range, cocooned from the seeking and penetrating dark by the light of Shanta.

Hasya and Devi this time travelled in silence. Devi had so many questions, but she didn't want to trigger any latent fears. Like what had happened to Vibhatsa or where Bhayanaka was. Or what Raudra had done now. And how long Shanta had left, which meant, how long did they have to reach her. Tranquillity was a reserve, packed in snow.

Hasya, who could read Devi's thoughts, said nothing in response. There was one more thing Devi did not know. Shanta was an air butterfly and Raudra, fire, was choking out the oxygen with her fuming fury. Shanta had even less time in the rarefied Himalayan air of the upper peaks, than they knew.

As they entered the opening in the side of the Tourmaline, the one sending out fingers of black veins to drink in the colour of the surrounding sister ranges, the darkness got even darker, it became Vantablack, the darkest dark known to man. Everything, even the sides of the mountain, the silhouettes visible in the night. This was as nothing as nothing could get.

Devi shivered. As the icy cold seemed to grab at her heart, she heard a moaning rising unbidden from her middle.

'Auuuuuuuuum'

'Auuuuuuuuum'

'Auuuuuuuuum'

The reverberation rose and with it, the memory of something that Ammamma had taught Devi one night a long time ago.

It had begun with one of Ammamma's *vidukathais* about the night.

"At night they come without being fetched. By day they are lost without being stolen. What are they?" Devi heard Ammamma's voice now, clearly as though she were sitting next to her.

"The stars," Ammamma said, laughing.

"I welcome the day with a show of light,

I stealthily came here in the night.

I bathe the Earthy stuff at dawn,

But by the noon, alas! I'm gone," Ammamma was saying.

Devi knew this one. "Ammamma, the morning dew," she said out loud.

Ammamma had one more.

"What is the answer to darkness?" she asked.

The question echoed in the cavern, bouncing off the walls.

"What is the answer to darkness?"

"What is the answer to darkness?"

"What is the answer to darkness?"

The answer came as a whisper in Devi's ear.

"The answer to darkness is to switch on the light within," Ammamma said. And then, she was gone.

Devi kept her eyes shut. She could see the scene as though it were right there in front of her. They were in the Goa house once again. It was late at night, after dinner was done, and the electricity had gone. Swarms of mosquitos had come at her with no fan to deter them. It was hot and muggy, and Devi awoke, afraid of the dark. She stumbled out of her room and came to find Ammamma, who'd been cosily settled into her recliner on the back verandah. She seemed to be content, humming a song, as she looked out into her backyard, the fruit groves, mango and coconut, in what then had seemed to Devi like pitch darkness. Ahead you could see the moonlight bounce off the waves, and hear the insects call to each other.

"Are you not afraid Ammamma?" Devi had asked, climbing into her lap.

"Afraid? No Devi. I'm not afraid," Ammamma had said. "I love the night. The darkness is just a sleep, a way to show us how beautiful the light, the awakening is."

"But there is no light to switch on Ammamma. They took the light away," Devi had replied, deeply concerned that it was just never going to come back on. There were no power cuts in Mumbai, so this was new to her.

"They can take all the electricity away, Devi. The light is not outside us, it's within," Ammamma had said.

And she had taught her how to switch it on.

"Close your eyes with your three fingers," Ammamma directed her.

"How does that make sense Ammamma? Anyway, there is no light," Devi had protested, not wanting to close her eyes in the dark. But Ammamma had made her do it anyway. So Devi had grumbled, but obeyed.

Devi covered her eyes with each set of three fingers. Ammamma then made her cover her ear holes with each of her thumbs.

"Now make a 'hmmmmmm' sound from your belly button to your head in one single breath," Ammamma had said.

Devi had covered her ear holes so hard she couldn't hear Ammamma and she had to pry her fingers open and whisper the instructions to her. Devi could hear them now, clearly.

"Hmmmmmm?" Devi had asked.

"Yes, like a buzzing bee. Imagine there is a bee trapped inside you and you're not letting it out, you've covered up all its escapes, and as you hear it buzzing, it's generating light and that is what is lighting up your insides," Ammamma had said.

Devi had done it. Sitting there on the porch in Ammamma's lap, her fingers covering her eyes, her thumb in her ears, she had hmmmmmmmed like a trapped bee, and inside her, like a thousand glow bugs rising, she had lit up, from belly button to the top of her head, like a living lantern.

"There you go," Ammamma had said. "This is the 'brahmari' breath, or the 'bee' breath. You're now your own lantern, your own source of power, your own electricity."

Devi saw the light rising inside her, and had wanted to gasp, but was too scared she would let the bee out, and so pressed her lips tightly shut and hmmmmmmmmed even harder.

Even when she opened her eyes, and it was all dark again outdoors, Devi had known then, the bee of light was trapped inside her, and all she had to do was look inside.

Sometimes, when the light went off again, Ammamma would call Devi and ask her to sit next to her and hmmmmmmm. "My personal lantern," she would joke and tell everybody.

Over the years, Devi had forgotten this, the inner lantern. Now that the darkness had come, Ammamma had reminded her. All she had to do was light it.

As they passed through the cavern now, Devi closed her eyes with her fingers, stuck her thumb in her ears, pressed down her lips and began to hmmmmmmmmm.

The hmmmmmmmmm rose at first like a pinpoint of light, growing to a glow bug in her middle, at first really small. As her hmmmmmmmmms rose in intensity, Devi saw the yellow stripes of the bumblebee separate from the dark stripes on his back. Soon enough, a whole swarm arose. Then, the bees disappeared behind their light, soft and reddish yellow, like a thousand sunrises over the beach.

By the time the turtle taxi pulled up at the secret landing wedged in a rock enclave off the cavern of Vantablack, Devi was radiant from the inside out and try as it might, the light couldn't be sucked out of her. Vira, Sringara, Adbhuta, and

Karunya, huddling over the bonfire glowing a soft saffron, pooled from the little courage they had left, even Hasya, next to her, gawped at her in awe and no small amount of pride as Devi pulled up in a light of her own making.

As the Rasas rushed forward to embrace her, relieved, charged by her presence, they regained the strength of their wings. The courage of their convictions brought the Rasas back, emerging full bodied, sparkling, and ready to fly.

"Let's go," Devi said, stepping on to land.

"Go where?" Vira asked.

Devi nodded at the mountainside that enclosed them, dark and ominous. They had to find the vein of courage, the glimmer of hope, within it.

"We ore for saffron," Devi said.

But how? Vira was all for picking up everything they could find - rocks, pebbles, stones - and begin thumping at the side of the mountain. Surely it would crack. But that couldn't be it, Adbhuta said. It would take days. They couldn't spend all their time mining. Time they simply didn't have. Bhayanaka and Raudra with Vibhatsa on their side now were gaining ground every moment.

Sringara turned to Devi, who was watching them argue, silently.

"You know this, don't you?"

Devi smiled.

"Remember Aranyanidevi?" she said. Sringara understood. They didn't have to mine the Vantablack. They had to request it.

"Show us," Sringara said.

Devi sat down cross-legged on the floor and began her Brahmari.

She covered her eyes and ears and clamped her mouth shut until the darkness inside of her was more than or equal to the darkness outside of her.

The Rasas followed her example. Then she began.

Hmmmmmmmmmmmmmmmmmm. Devi went. Three times. Until the buzzing of the bees pervaded her every cell, lighting it up, as though by a minute electric charge.

As they opened their eyes, they gasped.

Veins of orange and yellow ran through the hillside of the Vantablack like a finely woven web of light. Even in the blackest black, ran the slivers of hope by which the light could get in.

The darkness didn't matter anymore. The battle for the Rasa Bhugola was about to begin.

"What happened to Vibhatsa?" Devi wanted to know.

"Bhayanaka," Vira answered. "She got to her."

"Yes, but how?"

"By validating her worst fears, Devi," Hasya responded. "We told her what she could be, but..."

"Bhayanaka told her what she can see she is," Devi completed the sentence for her. "And it's far easier for

Vibhatsa to believe what she already has collected evidence for, so she went with that." It was easier to fall back into what people were telling you that you were than what you had to find the courage to be. Vibhatsa had taken the easy way out. It wasn't all her fault though, Devi knew, Bhayanaka's lure was hypnotic and Vibhatsa had been scared.

As Vibhatsa and Bhayanaka had joined forces, the Bhugola had first turned itself over to a pale blistering blue as loathing and aversion swept through the lands. Then, Bhayanaka took over. Bhayanaka didn't fly, she pervaded. Hypnotic pools of fear swirled out from under her wings, anticipating the worst of futures that did not exist yet, causing all who fell into its ambit, to become fearful and anxious. The darkness progressed into beings' hearts – little by little, worry by worry, concern by concern, what if by what if. Even as they sat and warmed themselves in front of their small fires of courage, hoping for the best but expecting the worst, she took over. In the darkness, the beings, perplexed, afraid, running for their lives, crossed the boundaries of the Rasa lands and lost their way. Even their most joyous memories became imputed with sinister intent. Their best relationships seemed now suspicious. Their fondest hopes turned to ash in their mouths before being articulated. They woke screaming with nightmares of falling into the depths of their uncertainties and ran out the door. The subjects of wonder strayed into the land of anger, and the beings of fear into the land of mirth. Consequently there was chaos and the lands were plunged into irretrievable darkness, their order and systems completely broken down. With Vibhatsa defecting, Vira wasn't even able to raise an army. Nothing stood in their way now.

Vira, in particular, was furious.

"Without Vibhatsa, Bhayanaka would not have infiltrated this far," she fumed. "We should never have trusted her and all her sob stories. It was all an act."

Rifts were starting to make themselves felt at the Rasa camp. Never before had the siblings been this divided. Karunya was all for mercy and compassion for Vibhatsa. Vira was all for exiling her.

Devi spoke calmly.

"If Bhayanaka would not have infiltrated without Vibhatsa, then it is by Vibhatsa we will reclaim territory too," she said. "We turn Vibhatsa against Raudra by using her fears."

Everyone looked at her.

Devi bent down and pulled chalks from her pocket. In her mind's eye, she considered the lay of the Rasa Bhugola. Bending on one knee, she expertly drew out the dots, and joined them, her fingers guided as if she had drawn this a hundred times before. When she had finished, she stepped back. The gathering of Rasas gasped. While they each knew their own silos of land, they had never before joined the dots, and seen how closely it was they were connected, or what separated one from the other. There it was now, clear as daylight. The entire Rasa Bhugola laid out for them, each of the lands a conch shell, skirted by sea and flanked by mountain ridges, connected yet distinct.

"And what's that at the centre?" Hasya asked.

Devi pointed out. "At the heart, the six peaks are Shanta's land."

"And surrounding it?"

"The inner circle is ringed by Raudra's flames, and the outer, by Bhayanaka's fears."

The Rasas exclaimed with surprise and wonder. So much of the Bhugola had been handed over to Raudra and Bhayanaka, no wonder they wanted it all.

"I will redraw the map once we are done, but for now, this is the reality," Devi said. "And I must take responsibility for the way it is. This is the territory we have to reclaim first, then, we can restore order again."

She turned to Vira. "Vira, I look to you to lead us in this. What is your strategy?"

Vira looked at everyone, and sighed.

"The only way to rejuvenate the Bhugola is by a Meghadhanush," she said.

"What is that?" Adbhuta asked.

Vira looked at them all. "We form a rainbow. We fly over the lands and we sprinkle each of them with our aspects equally. That's the only way to reset the algorithm that our disastrous siblings have broken down."

Everyone looked perplexed.

"But how?" Devi asked. "To form any sort of rainbow, we need Raudra. Without her, there is no completion and any rainbow we form will be ineffective."

Hasya agreed. "Raudra is a primary, we can't even create the semblance of her through a combination of the rest of us. There is simply no way to replace her."

Vira was all for staging guerrilla warfare, sending a highly trained team in, and abducting Raudra.

"What sense does that make?" said Adbhuta, "Even if we succeeded, which is highly unlikely, it's hardly like, Raudra is going to say, 'okay guys, I'm coming flying with you'."

Devi listened and nodded.

"Have we asked her?" she said.

"What?" Adbhuta stopped and looked at Devi in amazement. "Why? What are we to ask her? 'Will you please give us our lands back?'"

Devi smiled. "Yes, precisely."

Adbhuta's jaw dropped. "After all she's done?"

Devi nodded. "Here's the thing, we are not Raudra and we don't need to be... until we need to be. Until then, we are to be, no matter what the circumstances and provocation, determinedly ourselves. And who are we as ourselves?"

Karunya, delighted at this speech, raised her hand. "Compassionate beings?"

Devi nodded. "Which means..."

Adbhuta grumbled and kicked a pebble. "...We have to go ask her nicely first."

"So," said Devi, looking around. "Who will go and ask her?"

One by one the butterflies disappeared, turning their wings translucent until they merged into the Vantablack. Only Vira was left standing. She shrugged.

"I guess, that means it's just me then," she said.

Devi embraced her. Vira, glimmering saffron like a burning ember, the heart of a flame, glowered with a bit of rage against Raudra at her edges. As she fluttered her wings, a gentle rhythm of the war drums began to resound.

She nodded at the others and took off towards the exit of the cave. They watched her disappear like a shooting comet into the dark.

Devi paced nervously up and down the cave, guarding what was left of the glowing embers of their fire, while the remaining Rasas hovered up and down the river. There was no sign of Vira. What seemed like hours passed, though Devi knew in the Rasa Bhugola, you could get years of an emotion out of only seconds of love or hate.

Suddenly, a small flutter went up and down the line.

"What is it? Is she back?" Devi asked.

It was Hasya. "No, but there's a storm brewing on the horizon, come see," she said.

Devi hopped on the turtle taxi and they made their way to the mouth of the cavern, from where, over the cliffs, they could see lightning strike white and blue, and streaks of orange rise from the whirls of lava in the clouds. Their conversation was loud and unseemly. The whole Bhugola was rocked by the storm. The land shivered and shook with anger and fear and all the beings took shelter from the anger of the heavens.

"Courage, Vira, courage," Devi muttered to herself. This was not going well. Perhaps, she thought, it was all a horrible mistake to send Vira in unarmed.

As they watched, the flashes grew louder and angrier. Thunder rumbled across the skies, thumping its chest in arrogant war cry. They seemed to be arguing. At one point a flash of orange emerged from behind the outline of a vast dark cloud. Vira was pushing back with all her might. But it was no use. Raudra lashed at her with a lightning whip of fear and she was consumed by Bhayanaka swelling up and closing the gap again.

For a moment, the Rasas fell into silence. It seemed as though Vira had lost the battle. The landscape was consumed by the roving dark. In the distance, they could hear the trumpeting of musth elephants. Hasya shuddered and shrunk into the cave. Devi put an arm around her, but she was worried too.

"Wait. What's that?" Adbhuta said.

There was, beneath it all, like a gentle heartbeat, a steady rhythm of drums rising.

"She's alive!" Adbhuta cried.

"Let's go," Sringara said.

"NO!" Devi cried. Sringara would be completely consumed by the dark. If they lost Sringara, the Bhugola would never revive again.

Sringara turned to her. "We have to go together. That's the only way out. Raudra and Bhayanaka have her trapped in a *chakravyuh*. It's a pattern that will be her imprisonment. Vira doesn't have it in her to get out of it alone."

Adbhuta glanced at Devi.

Love and wonder; everything they had to draw their courage from. Devi looked at them. If she let them go, give their all to this, and they didn't come back, all would be lost. Forever.

Hasya took her by the shoulders and looked Devi in the eye.

"You can't let Bhayanaka take over. You can't let them win."

Devi shook her head. Hasya was right. Bhayanaka was creeping into her. She shook herself out, limbs and all and got back her focus.

She nodded at them. "Go. But hold hands. Go together. You are only each other's hope. If at any point you find your grip on each other slipping, you have to promise you will return, Vira or no Vira."

Sringara and Adbhuta glanced at each other and then nodded at Devi. They'd only get one shot at this. They'd have to get it right, or they would be spent.

As they streaked across the sky, a yellow and green, they sparkled with a combined light like a shooting star. For a brief moment, all the beings who peeped out of their windows to see what this green light streaking through what they would call the Night of Nights in the days to come was, were gladdened. They thought, maybe, after all, there was hope.

As they approached the heart of the conflagration, it seemed like the darkness consumed them. But Sringara knew there was only one way to do this. They had to forget about the enemy.

"Forget about Raudra and Bhayanaka? How? Isn't that the whole point of the battle?" Hasya asked, panting and puffing as she raced to catch up with them.

"What are you doing here?" Sringara had asked, turning around, surprised.

"If you think you're going anywhere without me, you're mistaken," Hasya replied.

"But the cave, the fire," Adbhuta said.

Hasya shook her head. "Devi is in charge now. She's got it under control."

Sringara had just shaken her head. This was no time to argue and Hasya was right, they needed all the help they could get.

"We'll just waste our energy and end up feeding them ours. Our focus is to retrieve Vira," she said. "Let's not forget our focus."

Adbhuta understood. They intertwined themselves around each other and streaked towards Vira, three times empowered by each other's strengths.

The bolt of green, white and yellow headed straight for the heart of the raging red and the overwhelming black.

As they entered the heart zone, the sky was rent with the cackles of hyenas and the trumpeting of the elephants roaming the plains. Bats flitted around unseen and unheard, their eyes gleaming in the dark, brushing past the sisters with their furry wings. Hasya clung on to her sisters even harder and shut her eyes. They would guide her. She trusted them completely.

The sisters flew like guided missiles seeking the glowing heart of saffron.

"There," Adbhuta shouted, pointing. "There's Vira!"

Hasya opened her eyes. Vira was entrapped in a fist of rage locked in by a glower of dark.

As they watched, Vira was slowly turning red from the feet up, the more defiant she held herself, the angrier she got at Raudra, and the more she was turning into she whom she opposed.

"She's turning her," Hasya gasped in horror, seeing what was happening.

"What do we do?" Adbhuta asked.

Sringara nodded towards the cage.

"We throw ourselves at her. Give it all we've got," she said determinedly. She looked at her sisters. "We can only fight with what we have, and that's all we have."

They heard Raudra hiss and spit all around them.

"Right," said Adbhuta, "so we ramp up."

The Rasas clasped each other tight and began to twist. As they spun faster and faster, they formed a bolt of lightning moving at high velocity. Even Raudra and Bhayanaka stepped back, startled by them. As the gap in the dark widened, forming a space around them, together the three sisters rose against the night and with a loud crackle, summoning up all the energy they had in them, snapped sharply at Vira's cage.

The flash reverberated through the sky with a blinding light and a sharp electric charge. As it pervaded everything, Raudra released the cage for a moment in shock.

Vira quickly unfurled herself from the storm and flew into Adbhuta, Hasya and Sringara's spin giving them the momentum they needed to move the other way. They flew out of the heart of darkness, a brilliant comet in the night sky, towards the Tourmaline.

They crashed into the side of the mountain in a heap and disengaged, spent, but safe and intact.

After she got them back into the cave with the help of the turtle taxis, Devi rekindled the fires that surrounded them in a web of saffron light, like tented mosquito nets to protect and heal their energy, and returned to her post at the mouth of the cavern. She stood there a long time, looking out over the cliffs into the darkness.

The lava swirled and the dark pervaded, but the blue light of the lightning flash, Devi noted, flickered like a tube light that had its doubts.

In the morning, they would rise against Raudra and Bhayanaka.

Vira was unharmed, but shaking with residual anger. Sringara had managed to elicit some reserves from Chaki who had gathered up a basket with cocoa, walnuts and cherries, bananas and mangoes from Sringara's land. They sipped the warming hot chocolate and ate the fruit now hungrily. Devi wondered if there was pizza in the Rasa Bhugola but it seemed an unlikely ask at this time. Adbhuta caught her eye and winked.

Three pizzas with all the toppings Devi could wish for appeared, including pineapple.

Devi's mouth made a big 'O' but she was thankful and hungry!

"Wonder of wonders," Adbhuta said, blowing her a kiss.

As they ate, Vira told them how it had all gone down. She had found Vibhatsa blocking her path to Raudra, and confronted her.

"How could you do this to us Vibhatsa; we trusted you, *I* trusted you," Vira had said. She had believed Vibhatsa would see reason with an appeal to her emotions. But that had backfired and how. Vibhatsa was tired of being played upon by her emotions, and she had wanted validation.

Raudra had seen the opportunity and taken it. Vibhatsa now went by the title of Commander-in-Chief of Raudra's army.

The Rasas tittered. "Army, what army?" Adbhuta scoffed.

Vira raised an eyebrow. "The army of musth elephants and cackling hyenas? That one."

Adbhuta's jaw dropped. "You're joking!" Hasya shuddered.

Vibhatsa, bolstered by Raudra's support, had snapped frostily at her twin. They were enemies now.

"You? Everything you are is because of me. You owe me, instead you command me sister," Vibhatsa had said, sneering at her.

Enraged, Vira had flown at her and Raudra had come to Vibhatsa's rescue.

"You are a thief," Vibhatsa had shouted as she had rushed at her, her swords drawn.

"Here, she is just another Rasa, just another one of us, and that's not good enough for her. There, she's somebody," Vira said, clearly pained by the encounter.

Sringara soothed her with a hug.

"So that's her game," Devi whispered under her breath.

"What is?" Hasya asked.

All the Rasas turned to look at Devi.

What was Devi able to see that they couldn't?

"Raudra is going to turn us all against each other. Each and every one of us. Thank you, Vira, sorry you had to face that, but that's why I sent you in, to get us the lowdown. Now we know their strategy."

The Rasas looked puzzled.

"We're going to fight them with the very weapons they are using against us," Devi explained.

The Rasas still shook their heads.

"Follow me," Devi said, turning on her heels. She led the way back out to the mouth of the cave. They stood there under the starless, cloudless, unnaturally dark sky. Still beyond still.

"What are we here to do?" Hasya asked.

"We are going to execute Vira's plan. In the morning, whenever that may be, we're going to make a rainbow," Devi said.

"With what?" Adbhuta asked. "We don't have Vibhatsa and we don't have Raudra, that's two elements out of seven, not counting Shanta. How on Earth are we going to make a rainbow?"

Devi smiled at them. "Do you remember what you had told me when you came to visit me Hasya? That I have a little bit of each of you inside me?"

Hasya nodded.

"There you go then. I have Raudra and I have Vibhatsa and I have Bhayanaka inside me. Use me."

The Rasas looked at her, thunderstruck.

Adbhuta leaned over to Hasya and whispered, "I told you she was a bit of a musth elephant."

Chapter 8

The Battle of Meghadhanush

The Rasas had no clue when morning was, the darkness remained unchanging and undiminished, but they were exhausted, and had fallen into a deep slumber under the gentle glow of the web of saffron above their head. When they woke, re-energised, they feasted on bread, fruit and avocado with honey, and almond milk shakes that Chaki had ferried them in his elegant picnic basket. The maples had sent their sweetest sap and the fruit trees, the last of their best fruit for the warriors. It was time. For everyone's sake, they had to get the day back.

The Rasas made their way to the mouth of the cavern and stood in formation.

Vira took up the first position, and would radiate the spectrum of violet, indigo and blue. Karunya reinforced the hearts of the beams with her modest bluish grey dappled with the gentle pips of saffron. Sringara came next, followed by Adbhuta, Devi stood in for Raudra at the far end, followed by Hasya, who would cover Devi in case things didn't go as planned.

They would hold on to each other and fly equally over all the lands.

"Remember, all, or it won't work," Devi had warned.

"Even Raudra's and Bhayanaka's?" Hasya had asked.

"Especially Raudra's and Bhayanaka's. The beings of their lands have forgotten who they originally were, they have been so consumed by rage and fear. They need us more than anything right now," Devi said.

"Remember that when you fly as Raudra you might get exaggerated in the lands she occupies. Give us a warning sign if that happens," Sringara warned.

"You will know," Devi said, simply.

She already knew the warning signs. She would get heavier and start to plummet to Earth. The other Rasas could strictly not break formation or the whole mission would be a failure. She would be on her own. Devi was careful not to say any of this out loud. Hasya, on the outer corner, bit her lip nervously. She swore quietly to herself, that whatever happened, Devi would not fall on her watch, and yet, she was so afraid that she might.

Bhayanaka was bringing the worst out in everyone, but somehow simultaneously, the best.

The six of them held hands, standing on the cliff's edge on the glistening Tourmaline range, and began to flutter their wings.

Hasya's wings emitted a gentle peal of chimes, and released a trail of starlight and dust, as though she had sneaked the milky way past the blacked-out sky. She was radiating a path enough to light their way through the darkness.

Devi, standing in for Raudra's range of orange to red, held on to Hasya's wing and closed her eyes, focussing hard on the one anger she knew would protect her always — Ammamma's passing, the loss of her old ways of life and the immense loneliness she had been feeling. She focussed on it, clenching her teeth, until her forehead began to pulse with a dull ache and all her repressed anger caused her to tremble again. Soon she was radiating shades of blue that veered into a deep, rich red. She felt Hasya's wing flutter gently against her arm as she began to veer into crimson.

On the other side, Adbhuta nestled her under her yellow wing, balancing out Devi's rage, sending off the chinking of the tambourine as she raised her wonder. It was impossible to move into a heightened anger as the mirth and the wonder balanced her out, Devi knew. But when they entered Raudra's territory, it would be a different story.

Sringara's flute trilled through the forests, waking the thirsty and hungry trees in the vicinity who shook their leaves in anticipation; the light would return. There would be food again.

Karunya's mellow violin strung their mournful thread of disappointment at their siblings' actions into a harmony of compassion as she reminded the troupe to send their love to those they opposed.

The drums thundered the rhythm for the rising as Vira, on the inner corner, to the left of them all, summoned disgust enough for what her sister had done, and courage enough for all of them, like a pounding pulse of the battalion.

The Rasas thought of each memory, all the words ever spoken, every view that ever enriched them. They were the guardians of all the beings that now populated their lands. They felt protective and determined to do them justice, to guard the valuable hues that depended on them for their survival. If they gave up, there would be no more wonderous beings, moments of joy, ripples of laughter, embraces of love flowing through the world. There would just be anger and fear and self-loathing. And they loved their worlds and its beings too much to allow them to come to that. They knew from the diplomacy effort of the day before that even brave Vira alone was not enough to combat this takeover. Raudra and Bhayanaka could turn any of them, if they managed to isolate them. They had already lost Vibhatsa, they couldn't afford to lose anymore. Even if the effort spent them in their entirety, they had to do this. They were fighting for their lives, but also, for those of every sentient being that depended on them. But most of all, Devi knew, they were fighting for her. For her inner world.

It was naïve of them to think that to exist was enough. Now they had to claim their territory, fight for what was theirs, demand their due, make space for themselves in this darkening world. The more they believed in what they stood for, the tighter the bond between them grew. They became unshakeable, and fused as though one, flowing seamlessly from one into the other, such that there was no difference where Sringara ended and Adbhuta began. They had become one glorious united beam of pure light. As they held hands and soared, something miraculous happened, a shining beam of white light shone like a sparkle through the parting path of darkness and encased them in a cool sheathe of fresh, crisp air. Devi gasped as the cool rays covered her, soothing the burn from the blaze of her red.

"Shanta?" she looked at Hasya.

Hasya nodded, tears in her eyes. There was just enough of Shanta left to encase them protectively. The ice caps would have melted with this effort, but now Raudra's flames would not be able to singe them. Shanta had sacrificed what was left of her to protect them.

They rose as one, the Meghadhanush, pushing back the darkness with the fullness of their strength. Rays of the Meghadhanush extended like a glorious light from them outwards and radiated across the heavens. A rare and wonderous symphony filled the firmament, trumpets and flutes, drums and tambourines, chimes and peals, as a veritable chorus of the gods rung out to herald their confluence above the roll of the thunder and the threatening clash of lightning.

As the darkness parted against the determined onslaught of the Meghadhanush, sprinkles shook from their wings like confetti and fell across the lands beneath them. These little drops showered love and wonder and mirth and courage and disgust and anger and fear, far and wide, dispersing them in the wind raised by the force of their passage. As the light spread, the mighty wind god, Varuna, emerged and began to propel them on his wings. As the sun god, Surya broke past a gap in the sky, he blazed like a beacon and forced Bhayanaka back even more. His rays used each droplet like a prism and distributed the speckles of the Rasas even farther than they had hoped.

As the Meghadhanush streaked across the sky, it shone with promise, so that all the beings across all the lands could see it and were filled with awe. It was powerful and mighty, no longer one stray emotion here, and another dislodged feeling there. Together, the Rasas knew, they had become invincible, a weapon of the gods themselves. They knew, when they saw the support for them, that they were unstoppable now, and little by little, the fear, the uncertainty that had gripped them, released their hold. As their confidence soared, so did they. Raudra saw it too and hissed and spat, not liking it one bit, lathering her rage until her flames licked even higher.

"Bhayanakaaaaa..." Raudra roared.

"Erect a wall they can't get around," she hissed her command.

Bhayanaka gleamed even darker. Vibhatsa flickered with aversion for her siblings. In her timorous heart, however, she wished they would deflect from her and not come to harm.

The Meghadhanush, buoyant on the wings of Varuna, and lit from within by the night's practice of Brahmari,

skyrocketed over the tallest flames and decimated the densest black walls until the light of Surya had penetrated and dissolved it all.

As the sky filled with exuberance, so did the land.

All manner of beings ran out of their homes, emboldened by the sight, and were filled with hope.

Devi radiated a quiet rage at what had been done to her lands and her people in her absence. More than any anger at even Raudra and Bhayanaka, she was furious at herself, for what she had allowed to happen to her, for the injustice of it all.

"Careful there girlie," Hasya giggled, her mirth back in high gear, "don't go all Vibhatsa on me now, remember to direct it outwards," she reminded her.

Devi heard her despite the pounding temper in her ears, and shot her a grateful look and remembered to channel her rage outwards, at the right targets again.

The glorious Meghadhanush floated down in sprinklings of starlight, galaxy dust, swirls of light and flashes of colour. As it began to shower the land like a vibrant thunderstorm, the balance of the Rasas was restored again. A rain of purple and pink hope cracked through the clouds and washed the residue of the darkness away. Parched Earth healed and burnt trees rejuvenated. Tendrils and saplings, grass and weed burst from the ground. The beings came out of their homes and cheered. There was dancing in the streets and a rush to get back to the lands they belonged to as the rain washed them of the soot and obscurity, and allowed them to recognise where they had come from. They had been wandering lost and across borders in the dark, not knowing if they were joy or fear, water or fire, all the same under the cover of darkness. As they looked down on the streets and fields, plains and hills, the wild horses began cantering along to keep them company, the birds rose, song spilling out of their throats, the eagles followed their trail, and the trees waved their wishes into the ether. In the seas the waves crashed their joy upon the rocks and cliffs again. The insects set up a mighty chirruping and the Rasa Bhugola was slowly filling with sounds of life again. The voices of laughter and the songs of rejoicing rang out across the streets. Parents carried children up on their shoulders so they could wave to the Meghadhanush as it went past, covering everything with its glory.

It was as though an eclipse over the Rasa Bhugola had lifted.

The darkness was pushed back, farther and farther, until it receded over the borders of the hills, kept back by the flourishing determination of Chaki's wards. They occupied the only two lands where it could now legitimately lay claim: Bhayanaka and Raudra's land.

"We mustn't let our guard down now," Devi called out.

Vira nodded in agreement.

The Rasas continued to hold formation. It was tempting to think the worst was over. But the truth was all the Rasas needed to be balanced everywhere they existed. So even as it had rained down love and joy and mirth and wonder, it had also rained down anger and fear and revulsion in equal measure. Each Rasa had to be available in just the right balance in every land to restore the algorithm.

Which meant they would have to push back the darkness and the rage in the two lands in which they were most dominant, while still adding more of these two qualities. This was dangerous. This is where they could risk losing Devi and Vira. Without them, the cause would be ruined, the battle lost. Without their realising, Bhayanaka had begun to creep up on them. The fear began to take over, sending a mesmerising darkness into their hearts. It was Shanta who noticed it first. She shuddered, gently, shaking them until the dark slithered and slipped off them.

Devi, intent on her rage, radiating the red in just the right balance, wasn't looking up. Vira, sensitive to changes in air pressure and any lurking enemy, saw Shanta almost slip off them and reached out to grab her. She held onto her with all her might. Of course, her attention was diverted from the path ahead which is what Raudra wanted.

"Look out," she shouted a warning to her siblings.

There was a gasp. The black was creeping between them. Bhayanaka had begun to stealthily line each one of them in relief. They each shook themselves until the black slithered off them and they fused together again.

Phew! They couldn't risk being destabilised again. The incident had shaken them, and veered them off course. They needed to regain strength. They had had to part with Varuna at the border. The wind would only conflagrate the flames of Raudra even more. Surya would make the heat unbearable. And they couldn't summon Indra to quell Raudra because he would aggravate Vibhatsa and spread the aversion. They were on their own now. Their speed had diminished considerably. It was important not to lose focus more than ever now. It was important to be surefooted and steady.

As they crossed the border, they heard a sound. It was a swoosh and the unmistakeable twang of the mournful lyre. Vira, guardian of the group, heard it first and looked around. She knew that sound.

"No, it couldn't be..." Vira wondered if it could be an ambush, but it was hard for her to distrust her own twin. She knew her heart, and she knew in her heart glowed the warmth of embers that united them.

Vibhatsa burst through the cover of dark and swooped into the formation, a brilliant burst of azure blue. She cut through the formation just at the point where Vira had extended herself out, transmitting blue, violet and indigo from her wings.

Vibhatsa knew, there was only space for one of them to be blue in the Meghadhanush, and the rightful blue was hers.

She sliced through Vira moving upwards from the jet stream below, unprotected now that Varuna had gone.

"Aaaaaaagh," Vira cried as Vibhatsa sliced through her left wing and passed clean through it.

The Meghadhanush lurched and tilted dangerously to the right, its left flank destabilised by the air and darkness now gushing through Vira's wounded wing.

Devi looked at Vibhatsa, enraged, the fury blazing in her eyes. She was sabotaging the whole mission. The Meghadhanush shivered and shook with Devi's anger.

Karunya fanned herself out to cover Devi with her wing, singeing herself on the heat, but holding her arm steady, allowing the compassion to flow through her, until Devi calmed down a little.

On the left, Vibhatsa was attacking Vira again and again, until her wings were tattered. This made no sense, Vira thought, even through her pain. She is my sister.

"STOP. STOP THAT AT ONCE," she shouted at Vibhatsa.

"How does it feel now? To have your wings ripped from you?" Vibhatsa asked.

"I never took them from you, Vibhatsa," Vira said.

"Ha!" Vibhatsa retorted. "Day after day, all you did was try to show people you were better than me."

"Why are you wasting time talking to her, take her down," Devi shouted from the far end.

"That's not true at all Vibhatsa, you know that's not true," Vira pleaded. But she was bleeding now, gravely wounded. They were passing through the heart of the darkness now.

Fear gripped them all, Vira most of all.

Would they ever make it through? Was this the end?

Was it Vibhatsa who would take them down?

Just ahead of them, they could hear Bhayanaka and Raudra roar with laughter. They had succeeded in turning them against each other.

Sringara and Karunya looked at each other. It was up to them now.

"NOW," Sringara said to Karunya. She nodded.

From within them spread a great burst of light, bright fresh green on the undercarriage and a deep, lustrous grey on the upper. Together, the rays spread out in both directions.

As Sringara's light spread through Vira's wings, they soothed her pain. The wounds and tears in the gossamer threads filled up, renewed with the light of Karunya's compassion. The cooling effect immediately saturated the Meghadhanush. It felt as though on an unbearably hot day, a monsoon cloud had gathered to lend shade and pour itself as balm into the cracks of the land. Sure enough, a gentle drizzle began to fall on the Meghadhanush.

"Indra!" gasped Hasya. Since Vibhatsa had crossed over, Indra, who had held back for fear of dispersing aversion through the Bhugola from the overcast side, never mind that Raudra was casting his thunderbolts around with frenzy, now seized the opportunity, and manifested. All that had been exacerbated was quelled.

Vibhatsa, who was approaching Vira for another swoop through, was halted in her tracks. Vira had shed the blue and shone a deep saffron now. Her bravery shone through heroically and there was no thoroughfare for Vibhatsa anymore. The raindrops of Indra had banded together to form a gauze-like spectrum of indigo, violet and blue, strongly woven as a net of steel. And she knew she could not dispel those.

Vibhatsa saw herself clearly in that instant, reflected in the multitude of drops, doing their job within the balance of the unstoppable Meghadhanush. The loathing and revulsion directed neither at oneself nor at others, but at the things that harmed the balance and integrity of the Rasa Bhugola.

Vibhatsa saw herself and wept.

And as she wept, filled with regret for who she had become, an antagonist to her own cause instead of the keenest and most courageous supporter of herself, a miraculous thing happened. In the downpour of Indra's rain, she dissolved into the rain herself. As she mingled into the shower, she felt herself released from the hold of fear and anger. She knew what was rightfully hers, and she was free to step up and take it.

She embraced Vira in apology. But there was no need. Vira always knew Vibhatsa had it in her. She knew her twin like she knew herself. It was her job after all to protect her.

"Vibhatsa!" Vira cried with joy.

Vibhatsa gave her a broad smile and reached out her wing. Vira made a little space, and Vibhatsa quickly merged into the formation. The Meghadhanush now felt a little more complete.

"I'm sorry I couldn't resist it earlier. I tried, I really did!" Vibhatsa said, shamefacedly.

"Of course, you couldn't," Sringara said, intervening. "How could you? Everything has finally been restored to the right proportion – love, joy, wonder, anger, courage, compassion, even for yourself. Until then it was just you trying to push the darkness back, and no one, not even we, can do that entirely on our own."

Vibhatsa looked relieved, so relieved that they all understood.

She turned towards the lands ahead with a sneer of disgust.

"Let's get them for what they've done to us."

A cheer went around the Meghadhanush. Vibhatsa was back. Which meant Indra was now fully activated on their side. And besides, he was really keen to get his thunderbolts back. They were going to wash out the fire that lay head.

As they flew over the Nilgiris, the blue mountain range, into the land of Bhayanaka, the darkness thickened like a viscous treacle. As they flew overhead, pushing into the darkness, their wings heavy, their pace instantly slowing, every forward motion requiring twice the effort, ever so slowly, the land began to push back the hold terror had over its residents. And they began to stir. Black tulips bloomed, and the serpents peacefully returned to their slumber. The black stallions raced the fertile valley of the terror plains. The sand glistened with ground pepper and the fragrance rose into the skies making them all think of pasta and how hungry they were feeling. And the sea to the left of the coast glistened like oil.

The borderlands, where the Tourmalines stood their tallest, now stood between them and the land of Raudra like a menacing fortress.

"Remember," Devi said to them, "it is not that you won't feel fear, but that it won't have power over you."

They each nodded. "Let's go," Vira said, leading the charge.

Vibhatsa, a sword newly minted from the forge of fear, knew exactly what to do. She had razor sharp focus now, and she enhanced the disgust her sisters would feel towards the fear. She spread the span of her midnight wings across the length of the Meghadhanush, tinting everybody a little bit bluer that they were. Urged by disgust channelled at Bhayanaka, Sringara subdued her love, Adbhuta her wonder, Hasya her mirth. Devi remained even tempered as she was, just the right amount of rage against those who were usurping her land; while Vira, newly invigorated by the return of Vibhatsa, burst through as though the darkness were merely another monsoon cloud.

Tempering each other, together they pushed forward. Since they had already been fortified against the fear within, the fear that was outside had little hold on them. As they flew, they seared the darkness until it began to scream. As they bore into it, Bhayanaka writhed like a snake in the grip of a charmer's tune and began to release a wail.

It took all the Rasas' strength to not be shaken off course. They had to hold the Meghadhanush even as they confronted their own sibling wailing in front of them. It was the hardest thing they'd ever had to do. They were assailed by self-doubt, self-blame, disgust, fear, loathing, rage and tormented by the anguish of their actions. Still, Indra rained down and Shanta kept them steady, and the Meghadhanush pushed on until the terrible screeches ceased, and Bhayanaka had coiled back into herself and silenced herself in deep hibernation in the wintry depths of the Tourmaline.

As the Meghadhanush passed over the shrivelled land, the circle it had rung around Raudra, it rained down a shower of love, wonder and joy, courage, compassion, disgust and anger in equal measure, in perfect balance. The glassy eyes of the howling wolves and the musth elephants turned, the mosquitos ceased their manic buzzing. Terror that had reigned the land was locked away. The beings of the land simply couldn't believe it. At first they came out and squinted at the sky, their eyes adjusting to light.

"What is that?" children who had never yet seen a clear sky asked their parents. The panthers glistened their gratitude and slunk back into the foliage of the now blooming trees, and the black howler monkeys and the lemurs chattered and swung among the branches again. The zebras sprinted across the fresh plains and jostled with the wildebeest at the watering holes again. Relief rampaged on a breeze through the land.

While the inhabitants were still fearful of this war above their heads, as the Meghadhanush pushed through, they felt as though terrified was not all they had to feel. It was possible to also feel some joy, some wonder, some love and that made the things they feared feel that much more bearable.

In the recesses of the Tourmaline, Bhayanaka was secretly relieved.

She no longer had to live in fear of herself. She could sleep in peace.

The Meghadhanush hadn't done its job yet. The blazing inferno lay ahead: the ring of fire that was Raudra. Jutting out of her heart, they could see just up ahead, Shanta, the ice all but melted from her peaks. And no way to reach her but through.

Chapter 9

The Thousand-Petalled Lotus

The Rasas knew if they flew directly into Raudra's ring of fire, their delicate wings would be singed. Unable to stop their momentum or break their flow, which would surely dismantle the potent spell they were casting to collectively push back the darkness, the Meghadhanush took a sharp turn and began perambulating the central rotunda of peaks instead. Raudra, who had been anticipating their charge, roared angrily when she saw them turn away, sending a tall flare spiralling into the sky.

Raudra had become emboldened by her conquest of Shanta. Without Shanta, the fragile air butterfly who was the basis for every breath that beings took, the Rasa Bhugola and its entire population, the entirety of the carefully-built balance between the Rasas would collapse. The whole world would become a ball of raging fury without her cooling waters.

Shanta had melted herself to lend her strength to the Meghadhanush, and the six peaks now lay bare and exposed, except at its central mound, a heap of perennial snow upon a tall glacier, on which Lotus temple stood.

As the Meghadhanush began circling Raudra's ring of fire, a brilliant red Scarlet Peacock butterfly rose out of the flames, her wings ablaze, hissing and spitting their music in a trail of glowing embers behind her, and made to escort their formation. In doing so, Raudra had begun to circle herself. She was so filled with rage and fed off herself so continually, she didn't believe she could ever be quenched. She had begun to believe in the myth of her own immortality. She began to encircle the Meghadhanush with a ring of fire.

"Steady," Devi shouted to the Rasas, who were starting to get quite alarmed, "scorched sky policy. Stay on course!"

Raudra flew close to Vira, on the inner circuit.

"Come over to my side, Vira," she beckoned. "You and I will take over the world. Fury and courage, what could stop us?"

Vira didn't even look at her. She focussed on maintaining formation. She knew what Raudra was up to, and she wasn't budging from her post.

Raudra laughed and dived away towards Vibhatsa.

"You traitor," she said. "After I raised you up. I have nothing but disgust for you," she spat at her.

But Vibhatsa was reinforced now, flanked by her sisters.

She returned the sneer. "Likewise," she said, and looked away.

As Raudra approached Sringara, to everyone's surprise, she turned her face away. After so many trees had been lost to Raudra? Not a chance. She would not forgive her, well not now at any rate.

That hurt Raudra the most. Of all the sisters who were obliged to love her, she would have thought, Sringara would not be the one to turn her away, no matter what she did.

She hissed and spat in anguish and the flames grew higher.

Adbhuta simmered at her sister on a gentle heat.

Raudra flashed a flare so bright that Adbhuta paled and whited out. Sringara and Hasya instantly replenished her with their yellow.

Despite her best efforts, Raudra had been unable to break the formation. She didn't understand what their plan of attack was though. They couldn't possibly take the flames. To be honest, none of the Rasas knew either, they were just going with the flow, intent on simply not breaking their path.

They were coming to the completion of the perambulation. Only Devi and Hasya were left.

Coming up on the right, supported by Hasya, Raudra saw that it was Devi who was standing in for her, this puny human with no wings, who couldn't fly, and who was more completely at her mercy than she knew when she went on a rampage. Perhaps it was the presence of Hasya, but Raudra began to laugh. She let out a thunderous roar, flames shooting this way and that, singeing the tips of Hasya's glorious wings as she went.

Devi, who had her eyes focussed on the Lotus temple at the heart of Shanta, towering above the inferno, heard it. She didn't look to the left or to the right. She kept her eyes on the Lotus temple, the heart of Shanta, upon which sat the three incarcerated goddesses, Durga, Lakshmi, and Saraswati.

The more loudly Raudra laughed, the more it infuriated Devi, who was already channelling her through a high degree of concentration. The more Raudra laughed, the more the conflagration roared and the more it leapt up and licked Devi's feet.

As they came back to the starting point of the perambulation, directly aligned with the Lotus temple, the sun stationed, luminous and scintillating like a flaming jewel, behind it, the Meghadhanush in front of it like a stringless bow, Devi looked towards it. Folding her hands, she bowed her head to the temple, and asked: "Ready?"

"What?" Hasya asked, startled. "Ready for what?"

Was there a plan they didn't know of? She glanced at Adbhuta, on the other side of Devi, quizzically. Adbhuta made a face at Hasya over Devi's bowed head, as if to say, "beats me."

"Not you," Devi replied, opening her eyes and looking ahead. "When I say so, release me."

"Release you? But... Devi...." Hasya began.

Devi was the only one of them who didn't have wings. She would plummet to the flames and perish in her own rage. Hasya couldn't... how could she ask her to do this?

Devi simply turned her head and looked at her, and Hasya knew, this was not the time. There was no time. Devi knew, Hasya realised, what she had to do. The Rasa Bhugola was her kingdom, and it was time for her to claim it.

"NOW!" Devi shouted.

Adbhuta and Hasya simultaneously let go of their hold on her arms. They clutched each other instead, closing the gap, hoping for the best. Devi began to plummet towards the Earth. The red streak gone, the Meghadhanush swirling as it was at high speed, began to fall apart. They looked down at Devi with dismay, watching her fall, the expression on her face serene. She fell like an arrow, straight, her feet together, her palms folded in front of her, her eyes fixed on them, her gaze pointed, and her lips were moving as though she was chanting something out loud, slowly, deliberately, mindfully.

"What is she doing?" Adbhuta asked, completely freaking out right now and frantically reaching for Hasya to try and keep the Meghadhanush circling. But it was already too late, the speed of their perambulation was so great, the rays were diverging this way and that despite their best efforts.

And then they heard it. A deep "Auuuuuuuuuum" arose from Devi, deeper than anything they had heard before, deeper than the rumble across the mountain ranges, deeper than echoes of the blue whales in the inky seas. Louder than the rumble of the ominous thunder, and sharper than the lightning bolts that rent the skies above Raudra.

As the chant rose, a gentle rain began to fall across Raudra. Indra was not angry, he was not anguished, he extinguished calmly, coolly, as he commandeered the rain, pushing the flames back as they sought to rise.

It was followed by the chant that Hasya by now knew so well.

"Karagre vasate Lakshmi
Karamadhye Saraswati
Karamule sthitaha Gauri
Prabhate kara darshanam"

As she completed the chant, Varuna returned, and swooped up Devi on his wings and she began to rise on the wind. Indra ramped up his anger, sucking it up from the dying flames and venting his fury across the land, pushing back Raudra's own as he unleashed a torrential rain across it. Surya emerged, radiant and splendorous, purifying the air, ridding it of the soot and smoke. Between them, the Meghadhanush shone brighter than it ever had, strengthened by their combined force.

The six peaked mountain range at the heart of Shanta began to rise of its own accord and heave outwards and upwards. It rose from the Earth as lightly as if it were made of air itself. Beneath the Meghadhanush, in a scintillating flash, the mountains absorbed the light of the sun and flashed them outwards, fanning out into a glinting thousand-petalled lotus. Each petal glimmered in mother of pearl across which was reflected every shade of the Rasas. It shone violet and blue, the spectrum of yellow to gold, shimmered pale pinks and luminous lavender, strident orange and the deep crimson of the loving heart. It stretched infinitely outwards through space and time and though the Rasas craned their necks, they could not see where it ended. They were captivated by its beauty, the awe inspiring, tranquil and majestic land that was rising, as it spun faster and faster. Their eyes were locked on the heart of the flower, the Lotus Palace, expecting to see the goddesses emerge.

They didn't notice Devi rise up in the air, standing atop the flames now in the command of Varuna. She rose till she confronted a stunned Raudra, face to face with her. Devi blazed a glorious saffron, a fiery orange, a brilliant yellow and a passionate red, and every hue in between that Raudra could ever hope to be reflected in her furious eyes. She had transformed into a warrior, holding in each of her nine hands, weapons of fury and rage, terror and disgust, but also love and wonder and mirth and courage and compassion. On her forehead she wore the lotus jewel, a six petaled stone that shone with the lustre of Shanta.

"You don't need to look back there," Devi said, in a voice that sung with thunder. She was no longer meek, or unknowing. She blazed with an ethereal light of awareness, that bounced off the mountain peaks and amplified through the petals of the lotus jewel.

"The goddesses are right here," she said, and simply, raised her palms to the front of her face.

As she did so, the flames beneath her swirled and turned into a shining discus in her hand of fury, still deadly and potent, but compact and contained. All of a sudden, the fiery plains emptied out, and the landscape returned to the cheery vibrant cherry red it was originally ordained to be. As Indra poured down and flooded the plains with water, the fire energy within it receded, allowing the blistered skin of its Earth to be healed.

There were no beings in this land who had been able to survive Raudra's wrath, so there were no cheers, no cries of joy and relief. The land would have to be repopulated.

Her excess powers gone, the fury drained from Raudra's face. The ugly twisting lines, the frown wrinkles and the menacing glares were gone. She looked very much a butterfly like any other, and on her wings sparkled flecks of green and yellow and blue.

Devi spun her discus round in her hand and threw it around Shanta's peak. As it whirred, it gathered the divergent strands of the Meghadhanush back together, and Raudra was sucked by its velocity into a tame but still vibrant band of red, that spun at the inner corner of it, sliding in neatly into place next to Vira.

Everyone, especially Hasya, heaved a sigh of relief. And of her sisters who embraced Raudra, it was Karunya who embraced her the most heartily.

As they spun around and around, faster and faster around the swirling thousand-petalled lotus, a flash of

blinding white light, with the lustre of the moon, released its wings from the heart of the lotus and rose, like a phantom into the sky.

Shanta had been liberated. A deep and lasting tranquillity reverberated across the Rasa Bhugola.

The air turned crisp and clear again, and the river flowed silvery and steady. Throughout the lands, there were cries of rejoicing, tears flowed, as the beings embraced each other with relief. It was okay to feel anger and disgust at what Raudra and Bhayanaka had done without the fear of being consumed by them. It was okay to direct that anger and disgust at the things they wanted to keep away from them, to protect themselves from harm and danger.

Along with the restored joy and love, wonder and compassion, the beings marvelled at their own courage, their own disgust, their own anger and their own insecurities. They saw themselves in their own light and they felt, after a really long while, whole again.

The Meghadhanush had mixed things up, and all the colours of each being were restored, not only their most dominant one, for they were no longer in the grip of one thing or another Rasa, there was within each of them a bit of all. They were now free to roam through the lands, like Chaki, who was delightedly scampering through his myriad forests and would not be seen for a long time to come, except in passing and occasionally.

The redwoods and the sycamores, the deodars and the birches soared into the sky, drinking in the sunlight. And the seasons were restored.

Hasya looked around for Devi, but she had gone.

"I guess she knows the way now," Hasya smiled to herself.

Epilogue

Mom rubbed her eyes and realised with alarm that she had overslept. Oh no, she would be late for work! She stretched out in the empty bed, groaning, and realised she hadn't slept this well in a really long while. Two parrots chirped at the bird feeder Devi had made and hung out for them. Mom smiled to herself. She threw her head back on the pillows and looked out the window, remembering last night, all the arguments, the raging, the storming, the crying. "Wow," she thought to herself, "that was something else alright." Perhaps the sky had moody days too. To see the sky right now, you would never know. It was sunny and smooth this morning, its abrupt tantrum had passed. The air was crisp and had been washed clean, and it smelled of fragrant Earth and clean washing. Suddenly, Mom's panic and rush just fell right away. From down the corridor, the fragrance of freshly brewed coffee wafted through the house. Mom swung her feet off the bed, put on her slippers and made her way to the kitchen. Pa was reading the newspaper. He looked up as Mom came in. "You have time to read now?" she asked him, teasing, as he poured her a cup. "My third one this morning, believe it or not," he said, cheerfully. Mom smiled. Pa sounded happy. Perhaps some time off was not such a bad thing, they agreed. In fact, Mom suggested that she take a day off too. Who knew, if she was in the mood, maybe even the week. That made Pa widen his eyes and reach across the table and pretend to check her temperature. Then they laughed and drank their coffee in silence. It was a peaceful silence though, not the kind when two people aren't talking to each other, but the kind when two people don't need to fill the gap.

"Where's Devi? Is she still asleep?" Mom asked.

"Nope," Pa said. "Gone to school." Mom made that face, you know the one, the pursed lips and raised eyebrows, but the one which said that she was impressed, not annoyed. It was amazing how many feelings grown-ups conveyed with the exact same two gestures.

"Wow, just you and me at home today hunh? Wanna go for a drive?" Mom asked Pa.

"Sure, but first, come with me, I have something to show you," Pa said.

He nudged Mom off her chair and took her by the hand to the front door.

There, neatly drawn inside an intricate trellis of dots was Devi's *kolam* for the day, a complex and beautiful weave of a lotus, one that seemed, depending on how you looked at it, as though it could possibly have a thousand petals.

As Mom got ready to head off for her drive, and got into the car, she said to Pa, "Is it just me or do I keep hearing wind chimes in the house, Sanjay?"

Pa shrugged, "Not sure, why?" in the way that Pas are always replying.

Mom looked out of the window and bit her lip. "That's funny, coz we don't have any!"

Acknowledgements

This book owes gratitude to many. My father, who cultivated a childhood habit of reading and stocked me up with every book he could find, and my mother, who taught me to read them. From their library came *Alice in Wonderland* and *Wind in the Willows*, *Matilda*, *The Secret Garden*, *Malgudi Days*, yes, but also K.M. Munshi's *Krishnavatara* series, the Brihadaranyaka Upanishad, the Rig Veda, and the Katha Upanishad, all of whose resonances you will find within. The idea that these worlds, ideas could be enmeshed, interlinked and made to stand together in a state of play came from there.

My teachers, Sri Satya Sai Baba, S.N. Goenka, Dzongsar Khyentse Rinpoche, Venerable Geshe la Dorji Damdul, Asha Pillai-Balsara, and the cohorts of these sanghas who contributed immensely to the conversations around and clarity in higher thought. Bibek Debroy, generously accessible to any query on structure, validity and meaning.

Jerry Pinto, whose dedication to the word and the studentness of the writer continues to inspire and correct my language and form.

My siblings, Gautam and Gauri, unflinching in their support. My son, Dhruv, for whom in the end all my works are written. Kanishka Gupta, friend and agent who puts fair faith in drafts decades before they are worthy.

Publisher Ajay Mago, for putting his faith in the vision of Devi. Shantanu Ray Chaudhuri, my editor, for seeing the world within this manuscript and putting the eyes on the stone, Purnima Bhattacharya, my editor, whom the book has been waiting for. My gratitude to artist Papiya Saha Singha for putting a face to Devi and giving the characters of the Bhugola form. And to the sales and marketing teams at Om, Subhadeep, Raj, Saravanan, as well as Ajay, Sanjay, Karan and Brij for their work in birthing it. Neha and Nabhi, Dr Mamata Shetty, Mimansa Popat, Dhara Shah, Kim D'Souza, Smita Barooah, Deepika Ahlawat, shapers of thought. My nephew Biko, the first beta reader, and my nieces Anushka and Mihika, who reviewed the original. An inestimable debt is owed to Dara Mehta, for his generosity with his art. This story owes its love of riddles to Rani, who would tell me vidukathais as she walked me to school in Kodai. And to my grandmother, Jayalakshmi, who was always there, and when she was there, you needed no other.